THE GUARDIAN OF MISTY HOLLOW

Patricia M. Bryce

This is a work of fiction. Names, characters, places, and incidents are products of the author's imagination or are used fictitiously and are not to be construed as real. Any resemblance to actual events, locations, organizations, or persons, living or dead, is entirely coincidental.

World Castle Publishing, LLC
Pensacola, Florida
Copyright © Patricia M. Bryce 2018
Hardback ISBN: 9781629899350
Paperback ISBN: 9781629899367
eBook ISBN: 9781629899374
First Edition World Castle Publishing, LLC, June 11, 2018
http://www.worldcastlepublishing.com
Licensing Notes
All rights reserved. No part of this book may be used or reproduced in any manner whatsoever without written permission, except in the case of brief quotations embodied in articles and reviews.
Cover: Karen Fuller
Editor: Maxine Bringenberg

Dedicated to Syd
Without whom this story wouldn't have an end.

Belfry family Tree
Thomas Belfry; born 1815; Founder of the Belfry Foundry in Chicago
Agnes Belfry nee MacFee, born 1820
First born son Thomas II, born 1840
Agatha, born 1843 (The First Belfry Guardian of the Hollows)
Samuel, born 1850
~~*

Thomas II
Marries Elizabeth Moore 1866
Charles 1868
Sarah 1870
James 1872
Anna 1874 (The second Belfry Guardian)
Edwin 1876
~~*

Charles Marries 1880, Mary Logan
Jonathan 1885
Harriet 1888 (The third Belfry Guardian)
Martin stillborn
Robert 1890
Ann 1893
~~*

Jonathan Married Williamina Brown 1908
John 1909
Winifred 1911 (The Fourth Belfry Guardian)
Albert 1914
Abigail stillborn
George 1917
William 1920
~*~

John marries Agatha Moran 1935
John the second born, 1938
Mary Kate 1940
Edward 1945
~*~

John the second married Martha Roberts
John the third
Mary Kate Married David James Logan
Constance
David
~*~

Edward Married Rose Ryan
Nora (The Fifth Belfry Guardian)

Chapter 1

"To my grandniece, Constance Logan," the lawyer droned on as he read the will, "I leave the sum of ten thousand dollars."

Nora Belfry stole a timid sideways glance at her cousin. Connie didn't look impressed. In fact, as far as Nora could see, Connie hadn't expressed any emotion except utter boredom. Aunt Winnie had been very generous to everyone so far. She'd remembered her nieces, nephews, and their children. Connie's lack of gratitude perplexed Nora. Connie sat, looking like she couldn't wait to leave. Nora thought she'd even seen her check her watch once or twice.

The lawyer turned the last page of the document on his desk. "To Nora Anne Belfry...." Nora stopped looking at her cousins, and turned her attention to the executor of the will. "I leave the bulk of my estate. My property, my stocks and bonds, and all my remaining worldly possessions will go to Nora Anne Belfry, who never forgot me." Nora held her breath. Had she heard right? Had he just said the bulk of Winnie's estate was now hers? What did this mean? What stocks and bonds? What worldly possessions? Property? Did that mean the cottage?

The man behind the desk looked at the assembled members of Winifred Belfry's family. "Any questions?"

"How soon do I get the cash?" Connie asked coldly.

Nora turned to stare at her cousin. "Connie," she gasped.

The dark haired woman in the red power suit stood out among the rest of the mourners in somber shades of black, blue, and brown. She glared back at Nora with indifference — no, make that vehemence — causing Nora to pull back in her chair. Connie's quick anger had always frightened Nora. Right now, she was sure that the anger was aimed at her.

Nora worried that perhaps her cousin was feeling cheated. "I know you must have thought she was leaving the house to you."

"That shack?" Connie's disdain wasn't hidden as she turned full face to Nora. "Now that would have been an insult."

Nora blinked; she couldn't have heard the other right. "Connie," she said softly. "How can you say that? Don't you remember all the great times we had, spending the summer with Aunt Winnie?"

Connie glared at Nora, making her feel mousy in comparison. "Great times? What great times? I hated spending summers in that shack, being dragged up and down those ravines and battling mosquitoes. It's a wonder none of us ever broke a leg or came down with encephalitis." She stood, knowing her stature over Nora was intimidating. It had just the effect Connie was looking for; Nora cringed. "And if you had a brain in that head of yours, Nora, you'd be insulted that she dumped that rotting hovel on you."

Nora knew she was expected to cower, to give in and allow Connie to intimidate her, and under ordinary circumstances she might have. Constance and her brother David had always known how to bully her, how to bend her to their will. Constance was the eldest of the cousins who had spent summers with their spinster great aunt, and with her charisma she was a natural born leader. David had been and was still her more than willing toady, while Nora was more often than not their victim. She had always excused it because they were family. The memories of her childhood, her summers spent at Winnie's cottage in the woods, had been precious to Nora…more than that, they were treasured. She had created an illusion in her mind that they had meant as much to Connie as they did to her. Hearing Connie's sarcastic accusation shattered those illusions once and for all. Scales fell from her eyes and she saw Connie's true self, just as Winnie must have. She didn't like what she saw.

"But don't worry, Nora; I'll get you out of this…just as I've gotten you out of every other mess in the last six years," Connie said. "It so happens, I've got a buyer for that run down property, and with the money from the sale we can finally get you into something decent in town." Connie's eyes narrowed. "All you have to do is sign your name…."

Nora couldn't believe her ears. "No," she said quietly. Slowly Nora began to shake her head. It was the first time she'd disagreed with an edict from Connie.

"I have papers all drawn up," Connie went on. Nora

realized she hadn't even heard her.

"No," Nora repeated a bit more forcefully, and this time the refusal got Connie's attention.

Connie stubbornly ignored the refusal. "You should be grateful to me, finding a buyer...." She began her usual logical argument, berating Nora, knowing that logic was never one of Nora's strong suits.

Nora stood up. "I said no," she said, louder and more forcefully than she'd ever spoken to her cousin. When Connie stared at her, Nora repeated defiantly, "I said, no. And I mean *no*."

Connie raised one brow. "You can't mean to tell me you're actually happy about this...so called inheritance."

"But I am." Nora smiled. "I am very happy that Aunt Winnie thought of me at all. I think it was sweet of her to want to give me her home. She knew how much I love that house."

The dark haired woman in the red suit shook her head. "She left you a *shack* that by all rights should be condemned, in the middle of a boggy, bug ridden swamp!" Nora could see the pity in her cousin's eyes, and she wondered how it was they saw the cottage so differently. "Think of all the disadvantages to that hovel. The plumbing alone will cost a fortune to have brought up to code, and you don't have a fortune. Do you?" The remark was meant to sting, pointing out once more that Connie's father had been more successful than Nora's.

"Connie," Nora reasoned. "It's not nearly as rustic, or as primitive, as you're making it out."

"It's not where an up-and-comer should live!" Connie insisted.

"I'm not an up-and-comer," Nora blurted out. "I'm not a big time, high rolling, wheeling dealing realtor like you. I'm just a little clerk in a locally owned bookstore. I don't need a fancy place downtown, and I don't want that kind of life."

"Don't you want more out of life than you've had?" came the inquiry with venom. "Don't you want to be something more than just a clerk?" Connie demanded. "You went to college; you got a degree. Why aren't you using it?" Nora had no answer. "If you're waiting for some knight on a charger to come over the horizon to save you, you'd better wake up, cousin, and smell the coffee. This is no fairy tale! Now listen to me...I'm going to sell that property, and you're going to sign it over. Do you hear?"

"No."

David leaned over the chairs in front of him. "Ladies, you're making a spectacle of yourselves." The lawyer who had read the will was frowning. Nora, ready to let it go, turned away.

Connie took a long cleansing breath. "You need time to think this over," she said calmly before turning to the lawyer. "So, when do we receive our bequests?"

"I've certified checks for each of the monetary bequests. Those present will receive them now; those not will have them mailed to them, or direct deposited," he assured her, and then turned to Nora. "I'd like a word with you when we are finished." She could hear an unspoken warning in his tone.

Nora nodded and returned to her seat. She prayed that Connie would be too busy getting her precious check to bother with her. For Nora, Connie's money-lust was like that of the thirty pieces of silver that Judas received for his betrayal. David never gave Nora a second glance, and she thanked the heavens for small favors. Her cousins' attitudes toward Winnie were disturbing enough, but the outright disrespect and avarice made her feel sick inside. She couldn't understand how they had turned out so greedy over the belongings of their great aunt, who had been so generous in life and in death.

"I want to deposit that check before it's worthless," Connie told the lawyer frostily.

The lawyer's dislike for the young woman before him surfaced. "I assure you, Miss Logan, Miss Belfry was far more solvent than you've any idea. These are certified checks…the money is there."

Connie gave him a smug shrug. "If she was so well off, why did she live in that hovel?"

Nora winced and closed her eyes, trying to block her cousin's words out. Misty Hollow may not have been a grand palace or a fancy townhouse, but it wasn't a hovel either. It was a well tended, well loved, spacious Arts and Crafts cottage in the woods. With her eyes closed Nora could see it so well, seated on a hillside that overlooked a pristine moraine, and far enough back from the road that the sounds of traffic were remote and muted. There were no street lights out on that section of the county road, so when the sun went down and the night sky was clear, one saw a thick blanket of stars.

It was there at Misty Hollow that Nora had learned about the constellations and shooting stars and night blooming gardens. It was a very comfortable cottage, as Nora remembered it, classic in its design. Winnie had even proudly displayed the original blueprint of the house on a wall in the reading alcove, along with letters and notes from the house's designer.

She had been there a few months ago, visiting Winnie, who was ailing. It was the last time she'd seen her grandaunt, heard her encouraging words and felt the real warmth of family. Looking over at Connie, Nora couldn't conceive of her ever being supportive. Connie was much too self-centered to worry about encouraging anyone else, including her own brother. She'd not the time to waste on Nora, who she'd always seen as beneath her socially and financially.

David and Connie's mother sat in a chair in the front row of the seats of those who had been called for the reading of the will. Nora's heart went out to her. She, too, was ignored by her children, who'd had little to do with her since her husband's death two years before. Nora's parents had not attended, as the journey east would have been too much for Nora's dad, who was in failing health. John Belfry, Aunt Mary Kate's brother and the current head of the family, hadn't bothered to show up. His son Jack was also a no show.

Nora leaned forward. "Aunt Mary Kate, are you all right?" she asked quietly.

The woman turned her head slightly. "Just sad, dear," she whispered. "Just sad."

"Is there anything I can do for you, or get for you?" Nora offered.

The older woman shook her head. "No, thank you, Nora." Nora now wished she'd sat with her aunt, something her own children hadn't done.

Connie received the envelope containing her check, and

so did David. She tucked hers into her Louis Vuitton handbag and looked at her mother. "Is there anywhere I can drop you?" The question was asked with an icy edge.

"I have my own car, thank you, Connie," her mother answered with cool civility.

Connie moved to leave, but paused by the chair Nora had returned to. "Think about it, Nora." It wasn't a request, but a demand. "Long and hard. I'll be in touch, and I expect you to be more reasonable." The hint of a threat was there, as it always was when Connie dealt with Nora.

Mary Kate Logan stood up when her children had exited, looked at her aunt's lawyer, and shrugged. "I apologize for their behavior, Miles," she said to the man. "I'd deny those two came out of my body, if I could."

Miles Benton nodded understandingly.

The stylish woman looked at her niece. "I'm glad that Winnie left the Hollow to you," she said firmly. "Don't you let that cold-blooded shark I call a daughter wrestle it from you. If she's got a buyer, it's worth far more than she'd like you to know. And you'll never see your fair share of that money. So you just hang on to it, like Winnie wanted you to." She gave the girl a wink before moving toward the door.

Miles waited until he and Nora were the only ones left in the room. "Well, young lady," he said, motioning her to take a seat closer. "There's a great deal for us to go over."

"Really?" Nora mused.

"Your aunt was a complex woman," he told her gently. "She left a good many instructions." He motioned to a document on his desk, beside the will. "Some of which are a bit on the eccentric side." He gave her a wink. "But, you know how unconventional she could be."

"I'm still having a bit of difficulty in accepting that she's gone, let alone left the bulk of her estate to me," Nora confessed. "I don't even know what the bulk of her estate consists of." She moved to the seat her aunt had vacated. "You said something about stocks and bonds? Is there anything of consequence in them? Will I be able to afford to keep the Hollow?"

"My child, your aunt was a bit of an investing wizard," mused the lawyer as he opened the portfolio. "I dare say, on her investments alone you will be very well set for life."

Nora blinked, then gave him a look that conveyed she found that hard to believe. Winnie was known to live a very simple life, taking pleasure from her gardens and her moraines. It was hard to envision her as a financial wizard.

"Winifred inherited a very sizeable amount of property and cash when she was about your age, from her aunt Harriet, who had the cottage built," Miles said knowingly. "Many of the furnishings in the cottage are from that inheritance. Winnie built her fortune from there. The artwork contents of the cottage alone are worth a king's ransom. Winnie had quite the eye for what would increase in value." He pulled out a page of the inventory of the cottage and estimated worth of some of the artwork. "Your aunt had all those insured, and the policies are still enforced; we've had them changed over to your name. As well as the deed to the property."

Nora read over the sheet, eyes widening as she recognized the names of artists and artwork. "Connie would die if she had any idea," she murmured. "She hated some of the statuary that Winnie was so proud of. She called the statues in the garden trash."

"All of the financial accounts have been transferred to your name," Miles went on. "I suggest you continue with the management agencies and banks she used; they are very reputable."

"All this is mine?" Nora asked, looking up in confusion. Realizing that she wasn't poor any longer took a moment before it sunk in.

"Yes."

"Why me?"

Miles leaned back and smiled. "Nora dear, who visited Winnie, remembered her birthday, and made sure she had someone to share the holidays with?"

"That was just as much for me as it was for her," Nora argued. "When my parents moved west, Aunt Winnie invited me to keep her company. She was kindness itself. Returning that kindness was natural." Nora shook her head. "I didn't expect anything from doing that…that's not why I did it." She felt defensive, as if someone was comparing her to Connie.

"For you, it was natural," Miles pointed out. "Not for everyone." He shrugged. "You and your cousins spent summers with her when you were kids. Only you returned after your teen years. Constance and David couldn't wait to have excuses not to spend time with her. Surely you didn't think she wasn't aware of their disdain for her." The older man gave her an understanding gaze. "I had your aunt's confidence in *all matters*."

Nora looked at the list of holdings. "I had no idea that Winnie was so well off. She never made a big production out of her status."

"She didn't live a showy life," Miles agreed. "She lived

well, but not showy. That nurse that had been with her was paid for by Winnie, not by the family."

"I just can't fathom her leaving the cottage and everything to me." Nora sighed. "Miles, this is just such a Godsend right now."

"How so?"

"The bookstore and the building it's in, including my apartment, have been sold," Nora confessed. "I was let go two weeks ago, and I've been looking for work and a place to live ever since. I have a little saved," she assured him. "Enough to get me by until I found someplace, but with days until eviction…. I was afraid I'd have to move west and beg my parents for a room." Nora paused. "I never expected her to leave the Hollow to me. Connie being the favorite in the family, I assumed it would go to her."

Miles cleared his throat. "Nora, the Hollow has been in trust for you since you turned eighteen."

"What?" She stood.

"Winnie always intended to leave it to you. She discussed the matter with your father while you were in the freshmen year of college," Miles mused. "She said when we drew up the papers that you were the only one who would appreciate it. She said you were the only one who had the vision to see it for what it is, not what it could be."

Collapsing back into the chair, Nora pressed a shaky hand to her forehead. "They never said a word to me. With Connie being the eldest of us three, I always figured everything would go to her. For years Connie has been touting her position as the eldest, and the fact that she was Grandfather Belfry's favorite. Well, that is after cousin Jack; he's the one who will carry on the family name and business."

"Connie inherited a great deal from your grandfather Belfry, as did David and Jack," he sighed. "Winnie favored you."

"I had no idea," Nora whispered emotionally. "But Miles, I can't begin to say how grateful I am that she did." She took a deep breath. "Would it be tacky of me to ask how soon I can move into the cottage? After Connie's demands of how soon she could get her hands on the money, I wouldn't want you to think I'm like her."

"Not at all, far from it," he assured her gently. "Winnie was hoping you'd take possession as soon as possible." He held out a set of keys to her. "Everything there; the cottage, its contents, even her old car 'Tin Lizzy,' is all yours. The taxes on the inheritance have been taken care of. All you have to do is move in."

"I don't know what to say," Nora whispered as she accepted the key to the cottage with shaky fingers.

"There is one other thing," Miles said, and then cleared his throat. "Winnie herself."

Nora blinked, "Excuse me?"

"Her ashes; she asked that you be custodian of her ashes, just as she was the custodian of her aunt Harriet's." Miles's face flushed a bit, and Nora knew he was embarrassed slightly. "I'm afraid you've inherited Harriet's urn as well."

The idea had not occurred to Nora…her grandfather was buried in the family plot, as was her grandmother. Her father and mother had graves reserved for their passing. Nora and the rest of the family had gathered at the family plot weeks ago, after Winnie's passing. "She's not buried in the family plot?"

"No," Miles said gently. "She was cremated after the graveyard ceremony, and her urn was delivered to me."

"She's here?" Nora asked in a voice that squeaked.

Miles pointed to a very stylish sculpture. "She picked that thing out herself a few years ago, made all the arrangements, and took care of all the expenses with a funeral home. Not even her nephew John knew about her arrangements." He suddenly seemed amused. "I think it's rather humorous that she was present for the reading of the will without anyone having the slightest idea. Again, that too was her idea. She had a lot of stipulations, and over the years I've learned to just go with whatever her wishes were."

Nora stood up and walked over to the sculpted urn. "How very like her," she agreed. "It's rather beautiful, isn't it?"

"She wanted me to ask you to put her on the hearth," Miles said, having followed the girl over. "She said she was sure you'd understand that she didn't want to be far from her beloved woods."

"She loved Misty Hollow," Nora agreed readily. "How could I deny her such a small request, when she's been so charitable and generous to me?"

"Winnie knew you wouldn't." Miles patted her shoulder. "She said of all the family, you were the most like her."

"High praise." Gentle fingers reached out to touch the smooth surface of the sculpture. "Winnie, I love you." She was surprised at how warm the sculpture felt, but she kept that to herself. "Can I take her with me?"

"Of course," Miles said, taking the objet d'art off the pedestal it was seated upon. "She's yours."

Cradling the sculpted urn in her arms, Nora sighed. "Thank you for everything, Mr. Benton."

"I was hoping you'd continue to call me Miles," he said.

"Thank you, Miles."

"Is there anything I can do to help with the transition?" he inquired.

"I can't think of anything," Nora said. "I don't own much personally. What my mom and dad left for me when they went west is in storage. My apartment was never big enough for much of anything. I only stayed there because it was just above the store, and it was inexpensive and not too far from Aunt Winnie." Nora shrugged. "I'm afraid that she was the only family we really kept in contact with after Grandfather passed. Uncle John never cared for me, and cousin Jack... well, I don't fit his social contacts. I don't even get to see Aunt Mary Kate as often as I should." The admission of her lack of connection shouldn't have hurt, not after all this time. But it did.

"I understood that you had been engaged once." Miles's voice was kind and understanding, not laced with pity. Nora appreciated that. "Winnie said that didn't work out very well."

"No," Nora admitted, "It didn't work out at all." She had no desire to dredge up her past, not even with Miles Benton. There were some things she didn't want to share with anyone.

"If there's anything I can do for you, anything you need seen to, I'm at your service." He smiled indulgently. "I do hope you'll keep us as your law firm, though you're not obligated to."

"Of course I'll be staying with your firm...Winnie trusted

you implicitly." Hugging the urn closer, Nora shook her head. "I'll be fine," she assured him. "Soon as I can, I want to get settled in, and I'll have my parents' things delivered to the cottage and figure out what to do with it all. What does not fit in the house I suppose I can store in one of the outbuildings that Winnie has on the property. Maybe even open the old summer house with some things."

"Well, the cottage is very roomy," Miles said decisively. "And you can afford to add on. I know Winnie did when she first moved in; that little solarium at the back was her addition to the building."

"It's a thought," Nora agreed. "First, I need to move in and get used to the place. Spending summers there is a far cry from living there day to day."

"I'm sure you'll be very happy there," Miles said with a contented smile. "Good luck, my dear." He bent forward, and like an aged uncle kissed her brow. "God bless."

~*~

An hour later Nora placed the urn on one of the packed boxes that contained her few possessions, littering the tiny one bedroom apartment she'd rented after she'd graduated college. It had never felt like home; it was even less welcoming than the dorm room she'd shared with two other girls back at school. There was nothing there that proclaimed the space as hers. The landlord, nice as he was, insisted that she not make changes, not even allowing her to put up her own artwork or change the colors of the bland walls. So instead of nailing and hanging, she'd placed things leaning against the oat colored walls.

The thoughts of leaving here when she learned that the

building was to be demolished hadn't bothered her as much as the trouble of having to find somewhere else that she could afford. Living here had meant there was always a little bit left over to sock away in savings. For years Connie had pestered her to spend what little savings she'd had to buy a condo downtown, and find a job that was more *acceptable*, one like Connie's. To Connie's thinking there was nothing that compared with living downtown or working there. For Nora, who had lived most of her life in the suburbs, the idea of a downtown condo was detached, cold, and foreign. She couldn't see herself in a modern setting; cold steel and glass held no warmth, no ambiance for her. She didn't enjoy the nightlife that Connie adored; she preferred the quiet of home and hearth, even if the home was a cramped little apartment over a used bookstore. Now home was going to be Winnie's cottage.

Taking a seat opposite the urn, she looked about. In a few weeks this place wouldn't even exist anymore. Any sign of her having lived here would be gone. Not even the memory would be left behind, and strangely she wasn't feeling a thing; not even regret. Nora had told herself that it was numbness; the shock of losing Winnie and the bookstore job and the apartment had all played into making her numb. That's why she wasn't sad this was all going away. She was certain that once the numbness wore off, she'd be...devastated? No, that wasn't the right word. While she would mourn the passing of her beloved aunt, she knew she would never miss this dingy apartment.

One hand reached out and touched the warm surface of the sculpted urn. "We're going home, Winnie," she said gently. "Tomorrow we start our life—my new life—at the Hollow." Moments later she was aware of the stream of tears that were pouring down her cheeks. For the first time in years she gave into the wave of emotions.

Chapter 2

The day after the reading of her Aunt Winnie's will, Nora carried box after box of her packed belongings down to where her vintage yellow VW "Bug" was parked in the alley. She had rented a U-Haul trailer for the day, as the boxes would have taken up more than all the room in the car. In spite of not owning much, the small trailer was nearly full when she finished. She was the last of the tenants to leave the building. The elderly lady who had lived in the apartment beneath her had been moved out weeks before by her son and daughter as soon as the notice had come. The bookstore had been closed, and the stock sold off to bargain book sellers. She had called the new owners of the building earlier that morning to let them know she was vacating. When she finished it was just after two in the afternoon, and the building agent showed up to get the keys from her.

"All cleared out?" he asked coarsely, a half smoked cigar hanging from his thick lips.

"Yes." She handed the key over without hesitation. "The phone was turned off yesterday, and I paid the last gas bill."

"Bet you're sorry to see the old place go," he mused.

"Not really," she said with a shrug. "It was just a place to hang my hat. It was never really home."

He nodded, and wished her well.

Getting into the car, she took one last look at the alley and the backs of buildings that had been her "backyard," so to speak, since she'd moved in. Most of the block was empty now. The old houses behind her had been gutted for salvage, and were ready to be given the ball. Two had gone down earlier that week. In a few weeks the entire block, front and back, would be nothing more than rubble awaiting a new life. So much of her home town was going through this modernization and renewal. Old buildings vanished, new ones went up, and no one seemed to notice the disappearance of what had been neighborhoods.

Nora wished she could muster some kind of feeling of remorse at seeing this place go. She had been far more upset when her parents had sold her childhood home, so upset that to this day she refused to drive in that area of town. It was silly, she knew, but she just couldn't bear the thought of someone else in her mother's kitchen. Or someone else's car in her father's garage. And the very thought of someone else in her bedroom was too much to bear.

Her mother and father had been gone for five of the six years she'd lived over the bookstore, but she was still obsessing over a house she couldn't have afforded. Not that she'd ever given a thought to living in that house. Not even when Daniel had asked her to marry had she thought about living in her mother's house. She couldn't see him in the modest little residence that had been home to her during her formative years. Daniel was much too much like Connie; he wanted the bright lights and dazzle of the city. Little wonder they were such a bad fit. He would never have enjoyed the quiet life that the woods afforded, and more than Nora loved her parents' place, she loved the cottage.

Turning the car onto the main street of the little town, she headed west toward the little country highway that would take her to Winnie's cottage out in the woods. On a good day it usually took half an hour to travel. On a bad day it could be as long as an hour and a half or two. She remembered one winter when, after not being able to reach Winnie, she'd driven nearly four hours to reach the cottage, only to find the old woman sitting in the parlor with a roaring fire. She'd spent the rest of that night and more than half the next day with Winnie. Today was a very good day. Being a workday, the traffic going out of the little town was relatively light, and the traffic signals seemed to be with her. A rush of exhilaration swept through her. She was going *home*, and bringing Winnie back home as well.

She'd last been out to the cottage on May Day, to bring Winnie a potted plant for her ever growing collection of plants on her tiered patio. Years before Nora had been born, Winnie had turned the hillside into her private rock garden and raised beds. What had begun as haphazard had turned into a floral waterfall effect garden that seemed to spill out of the Victorian style green house solarium at the back of the Arts and Crafts cottage. Most of the plants were either indigenous or things that were impervious to harsh Midwestern winters.

Year after year it was added to until the entire embankment was covered, always leaving room for the herbs and veggies that Winnie home grew every summer. Right up to the end she was Winnie.

Winnie had been sitting on the patio when Nora had arrived with the potted plant. Her hired nurse was upset that the daily schedule was being altered with the visit. Winnie cheerily offered to dismiss the woman. Nora had moved past the pinched-nose, white-uniformed woman to hug her aunt. At ninety-eight, the old woman had been deceptively youthful in appearance, often mistaken for someone a good many years younger. Her snow white hair was always worn in a braided bun and pinned up at the top of the back of her head. Her cheerful green eyes looked over Ben Franklin specs seated on cheeks that were smooth as a baby's behind. Nora envied her complexion, and hoped her own would wear as well over the years. Her voice was strong and without hesitation as she greeted her niece.

"Nora dearest, how wonderful! And you're just in time for tea." It had been a private ritual that had started long ago, tea on May Day. Winnie looked forward to all of Nora's visits, but the one on May Day most of all. They had spent the afternoon in the gentle breeze, enjoying the warm sunshine and the promise of the spring and summer that was to come. Only a few weeks later, Winnie was gone, having died peacefully in her slumber, the hint of a smile upon her lips.

As the yellow "Bug" drew closer to the famous area of moraines, Nora became excited. When she was a child and her parents would drive her out to the cottage for her weeks with Winnie, she'd felt this same rush of joy. The cottage had always felt like home, and returning each year had been something she'd looked forward to. When she was a teenager and Connie had taken a job and David had insisted on going to a boy's camp with friends, it was just Winnie and Nora. The days were filled with hiking and learning the plants in the woodlands and the wetlands of the Hollow. Fishing in the little stream that ran through the property. Watching the migratory birds that often stopped there on their way to somewhere Nora had never been. Nora was certain she prized those few years most of all. She'd always felt guilty about that, that she'd enjoyed her time alone with Winnie much more than the times she had to share her with cousins. She would never have said so for fear of hurting Connie's feelings. She wondered now why she'd been so worried about that, when it was so clear from yesterday that Connie couldn't have cared less. It hurt that Connie was so indifferent, and Nora felt insulted for Winnie.

The gentle roll of the hillside gave way to odd shapes and gullies with sudden dropoffs. Pockets of forest preserve land were on either side of the roadway, all part of the great Moraine Valley. The road snaked past Buttonbush Slough, where cranes were teaching their young how to survive in a world that was no longer theirs alone, turning south to pass the remains of the Swallow Cliffs, where toboggans once sped down the winter hillside, and now a nature trail stood out. Just before reaching Papoose Lake she turned to go west. There, nestled between forest preserve and greenery, was the entrance to the acreage that had been handed down from a Belfry aunt to a Belfry niece for going on five generations. Misty Hollow had well over one hundred and fifty acres, and the only neighbors for a good two miles in any direction were the flora and fauna. There were only a few homesteads similar to Misty Hollow, held in families until they died out, leaving the land to the county to be incorporated into the Forest Preserve. So far, the Belfry family didn't show signs of dying out.

For Nora, seeing the house at the end of the long winding drive was like seeing a glimpse of paradise. The cottage almost looked like something from a Thomas Kincaid painting; it could have been the base for one of his famous rural scenes. It was the kind of house that summoned up thoughts of gingerbread and sugarplums, or little girls in red cloaks, or wolves that would threaten to huff and puff. It had fired up so many fairytale dreams for Nora when she'd been a child here.

Nora parked, stepped out of her car, and took in everything; the smells of the forest that surrounded her, the sounds of the birds, whose songs were as individual as each bird was. Nora knew them all. In her distant memory she could hear Winnie calling out to her and the cousins, greeting them as they arrived for their annual visit.

"I'm home," she closed her eyes and said aloud with a rush of emotion. "I'm really home."

She opened her eyes, took out the set of keys that Miles Benton had given her, and marched up to the front door. Turning the largest key in the lock, the door opened with ease. Stepping into the foyer, she looked about the generously portioned room that opened into the airy parlor. The white wainscoting paneling and the soft yellow of the walls of the parlor were classic. Winnie's taste in furnishings leaned toward colonial and traditional, much like Nora's own tastes.

The richness of the fabrics and the textures were so familiar. The scent of flax soap and lemon oil from spring cleaning still filled the air. Art was on the wall, and not a speck of dust was to be found. She felt as if she had come home after a long journey.

She couldn't imagine Connie living in this kind of house. This was lace curtains and doilies, wingback chairs with vibrant colonial print upholstery and elegant wooden accents. Even though the house had been closed up for almost six weeks since Winnie had passed, the air was fresh, and the rooms still felt lived in. With the August sunlight streaming in the windows, it was paradise.

Nora quickly returned to the car, pulled the sculpted urn from the front passenger's seat, and carried it lovingly into the house. "You're home, Winnie. You wanted to be on the mantle, on the mantel you shall go." Her fingers gently moved a couple of knickknacks over to make room for the burial vessel. The ebony colored material of the urn in the wave contour should have looked completely out of place, but it didn't. It melded into the décor like it had always had a place there in the scheme of things. She planned to find Aunt Harriet's urn and place it there as well.

Nora stood back, just looking for a moment at the placement before she went about the business of unpacking the back seat of the car and the rented trailer. She finished carrying the boxes upstairs and left them piled in the back storage room. She had nothing but time for right now, and thanks to Winnie she didn't have to settle for just anything anymore. She could give some thought to what she wanted to do with the rest of her life. A call to Miles would give her a better take on just where she stood.

The cooler that had held the remains of her refrigerated food had been emptied and put away. She made a list of what she was going to need food-wise, and planned a quick shopping trip as soon as she had the trailer returned to the rental. Satisfied that she'd done as much as she could, she locked up the cottage. She closed up the trailer and prepared for the drive back. She was glad she wasn't going to have to spend several days getting all her accounts changed over to the new address. But it was too much to think about for now. Right now she had to get the trailer back and get some supplies in for supper.

~*~

It was twilight when she returned to the cottage. In the late afternoon the house seemed to have a rosy glow. This time instead of parking in front of the cottage, Nora pulled her VW to the back where the carriage house stood. She carried the boxes with groceries up to the back porch and left them on the enclosed porch floor before parking her car in the carport attached to the garage that housed "Tin Lizzy," Aunt Winnie's immaculate old car.

The kitchen was spotless, as was the rest of the house, and for the first time Nora wondered if Mr. Benton had hired someone to do a thorough cleaning before he'd turned the keys over to her. There wasn't a speck of dust or grime anywhere. And the house didn't have that telltale stale air smell that accompanied any place that was closed up. She frowned, thinking about the oddity and putting the supplies away. She began to investigate the contents of items already in the cupboard. Gently she tapped her fingers on the counter as she gave a more careful inspection.

"That's so odd," she remarked to herself. "It's as if someone replenished the pantry."

Mr. Benton hadn't mentioned having done so, and she wondered if the nurse had before she'd left the day after Winnie passed on. But then, why would she? The grumbling of her stomach took precedence over her apprehension or her concerns.

She remembered that Winnie usually ate in the kitchen, saving the pretty dining set off the parlor for special occasions. Sundays, holidays, and birthdays were made to feel all the more out of the ordinary because of her aunt's habits. The cottage's kitchen was large, airy, and comfortable. The soft buttercup-yellow paint on the walls gave the warm cozy feeling associated with the homines of a Rockwell painting. The walls held aged copper jelly molds and wooden utensils. Little shelves held Winnie's collection of salt and pepper shakers. In the center of the room stood the enameled double drop leaf table, with its cream colored background and its tan design of wheat shafts and ribbons. It was as familiar to Nora as her own face, and had been in this kitchen for the better part of fifty years. The wooden Windsor and ladderback chairs pushed against the wall gave the room an inviting coziness. Nora remembered spending many hours at this table, eating meals, playing card and board games on rainy days, and just enjoying a nice afternoon cup of tea from one of Aunt Winnie's whimsical tea pots. Winnie had enjoyed collecting numerous items—teapots, spoons, art—and all of the items made the house feel homey.

Preparing her evening meal, Nora thought about the fact

that her entire apartment—well, most of it—would have fit into the space of this kitchen alone. The two little apartments that were over the bookstore had been added as afterthoughts. Originally they were storage and office space, and had been within her means. She had lived frugally, not asking for help from family. Not that help from her extended family had ever been offered. Uncle John treated her like she didn't exist most of the time. After her parents had moved out of state, invites to the family homestead had stopped. Not surprising was the fact that Connie made a great fuss over having been invited to family occasions there, always with the snide, "What a pity you weren't invited." Instead Nora had been left on her own, in that cramped little glorified space that her landlord referred to as a studio apartment. It had meant that she couldn't squeeze in any of the few things that her parents had left for her. Furnished apartments that were economical were not in abundance, and Nora knew she'd been lucky to get it when she did.

She ate her first meal in silence, not even switching on the radio that Winnie had sitting on a shelf over the counter. All she wanted right now was peace, quiet, and space.

The sun had set, and the hills still had the rosy glow of dusk bathing them. Nora washed up her few dishes and put them to dry in the rack on the counter. Nothing had changed much. Only the woman doing the chores had been replaced. Nora remembered all the little rituals that Winnie would perform, and when she was the only one who was spending the summer months with the aging woman, she'd performed them as well. Winnie had taken many hours to instruct and coach Nora on the exact manner of performing each task.

Now the adult who had spent more time here as a child than the others began to execute the task of putting straight the heart of the house as she'd been taught.

As if following the instructions of a voice from the distant past, Nora moved to the little door that hid a small utility closet. Hanging up was Winnie's white apron with the delicate dotted Swiss ruffles. She tied it on just as she'd seen Winnie do countless times. Then automatically she reached for the corn broom. It wouldn't budge. Nora frowned, and pulled harder. It still stayed within the clip that held it to the inner wall. Her frown deepened as she put both hands on the broom and gave it a violent yank, only to fail to make it budge.

She inspected the mechanism on the clip. It seemed simple enough. She'd moved closer to get a better look when the broom suddenly shot off the clip and smacked her on the head with its long, hardwood handle. Nora, stunned, backed away and cried out. The broom followed her and smacked her again, just as hard and just as sharply. Startled and defensive, she put up her hands to protect herself as the broom came forward as if to attack her. Somewhere in her mind, she knew that wasn't possible. Yet here she was being driven away from the broom closet by Winnie's broom. Nora moved back, expecting the broom to fall to the ground, but it didn't fall…it rushed forward in full attack mode.

The broom's bristles began to shift as it marched aggressively across the floor at her. Nora stared at it. "You can't do that!" she declared, but the broom continued to press forward, chasing her out of the kitchen and into the parlor as if she were an intruder and it was protecting its space. Behind the broom Nora could see the old string mop that Winnie had used following, along with other items from the little utility closet filing out behind the broom. "This isn't happening," she said loudly. But the household cleaning supplies continued to mount their assault. Windows began to rattle, and shadows danced across the old polished hardwood floors. The old bentwood rocker began to rock violently to and fro.

Nora was certain she'd lost her mind as she backed across the floor with her hands held out to prevent the broom from injuring her with its deadly accuracy. She had backed herself up to the door and opened it up in order to flee the offense of the attack force. When the door opened a voice greeted her.

"Guardian of the Misty Hollow; greetings."

The sound drew her attention away from the broom and its companions. She turned to look at the place the sound was coming from. On the porch stood a man, tall and lean and dressed in shades of blue and green and gold medieval garments. While he was not young, neither was he old, and his being clean shaven meant she could see the fine sharpness of his features. His almond shaped eyes with their narrow, pointed brows looked out of time and place, as did his outlandish manner of dress. He bowed to her with a flourish, with hat in hand.

"You look like a refugee from a Renaissance Fair," she muttered just before she received a sharp rap from behind, and everything fell into velvety blackness.

Chapter 3

As the darkness lifted Nora heard a voice talking to her. "Guardian.... Guardian.... Oh dear.... Do awaken...."

She didn't recognize the voice or the accent, but she didn't feel alarmed as she opened her eyes; what she felt was annoyed. "Where am I? Who the hell are you, and...what the hell just happened?" She forced her eyes to focus.

"Thank the Gods," the effeminate man said as he patted her hand in his rapidly. Even with her unfocused vision she could see the slender visitor seemed unusually panicked. "Guardian, you mustn't frighten me so," he scolded.

Putting a hand to the lump at the back of her head, she grumbled, "Frighten you?"

"Indeed," he replied. "Surely you were expecting me."

Pulling away from his unsolicited help, she glared at him. "Think again." She shook her head slowly, as it was too painful to make quick movements. "I have no idea of who you are, or why you keep calling me Guardian. My name is

Nora." She glared at him, hoping it would put him off.

The man's face registered insult and anguish. "No idea?" He sounded as if he didn't believe her, as his baritone voice raised an octave. "Why, I'm Robyn…Robyn Goodwyn, of course." His voice was agitated, and he looked like he was about to pitch a childish fit or demand an apology.

"I don't know any Robyn Goodwyn," she argued as she tried to rise up off the porch, but only came to rest on her knees.

"Didn't Winnie tell you I'd be coming?"

"Winnie died in June," Nora answered.

"Yes, I know, that's why I'm here. Surely you've been expecting me!"

"You know she died?"

"Of course," he declared petulantly. "That's why I'm here…didn't I just say that?"

Nora blinked. "Why?"

"To help you," he said exasperatedly.

"Help me what?" she asked.

"Make the transition." His voice rose and he shook.

"I think I can move in without the help of…. What are you, anyway?" Nora demanded.

"*I am Robyn Goodwyn*," he answered, as if that was supposed to tell her all she needed to know.

"You said that before."

He stared at her with the bluest eyes she'd ever seen. And for the first time in her life, Nora found she didn't like blue eyes or being stared at.

"Look fella, I don't know who you are, or why you're here—"

"I'm here to help you make the transition," he insisted harshly and insistently.

Nora took a long ragged breath. "Transition?"

"Of course." He nodded rapidly.

The young woman pulled herself up to a seated position on the porch, and held up her right hand. "What transition?"

"To Guardian, of course."

"Guardian?"

He nodded rapidly again.

"Of what?"

"Misty Hollow." He waved a long elegant hand about at the woods.

"Is this a joke?"

"Do I look like a jester?" he asked.

She nodded. "Yeah, a bit." She stared at him. "Are you some kind of singing telegram? Or entertainment thing? Because if you are, I really don't have time. I've a situation in the house I need to take care of. And I'm on the verge of losing my mind, so if you don't mind...."

The man blinked. "You really have no idea of who I am, do you?" He appeared to be very distressed by the realization.

"Nope," she said curtly.

Long narrow fingers covered the shapely features on the male face. "This is not possible."

"Look, I thank you for the entertaining greeting, and the well wishes...." Nora felt strong enough to try to rise to her feet, and did so carefully. "But it's been a very trying day, and I'm having enough trouble with hallucinations already. So say your piece and go."

"Go?" He made a face as his hand dropped away. "How

am I to go before I even begin to assess your trained skills? Guardian, are you mad?"

"I'm getting there." Nora made a face that echoed his. "What trained skills?"

"The skills of the Guardian. How are we to assist you if we don't know where you are deficient?" he asked, as if she should understand what he was speaking of.

"What the hell are you babbling about?" She pointed toward the front door. "Look, I'm having a nervous breakdown. You're most likely some silly figment of my imagination, just as the broom and mop attacking me was." She laughed. "You're not even really here."

Robyn blinked. "The broom and mop attacked you?"

"No, I imagined they attacked me," she argued. "Brooms don't go about attacking people...and why am I discussing this with you? You don't even exist, you're just a figment."

Reaching forward, he sharply pinched her arm. When she yelped he said, "I assure you, Guardian, I do exist."

Rubbing the now pained place on her arm that was sure to bruise, Nora growled, "Was that necessary?"

"Yes," he said, and then sighed. "You said the broom and mop attacked you."

"I said I imagined it," she argued. However, the lump on her head and the pain from being struck said differently. Not that she was about to tell this...person that.

Robyn shook his head. "This is not a very good start, Guardian, if your own broom won't accept you."

"It's not my broom," she said harshly. "That's Winnie's broom...and her mop...and her—"

A hand placed on her lips silenced her. "Oh, dear," the man

sighed. "This is not good at all." Nora stared at the hand that was silencing her lips. The man seemed to be contemplating something that was very important. "So, Winnie didn't tell you anything of what to expect on your first eve in the domicile of the Guardian?" he asked at last.

Nora shook her head in the negative.

"Oh, dear."

Removing his hand from her lips, Robyn then began to tap the long fingers to his own chin. "How can this be?" he said to himself, as if Nora no longer existed for him. "How could she leave things so undone? I've never known her to be so…careless. Except that once, but that couldn't have anything to do with this." The rhythm of the fingers tapping stopped abruptly. "Or could it?" Nora had seen men fret like this before.

While the man was deep in thought and private conversation with himself, Nora edged her way back to the front door, planning on barring herself within. When she turned the handle and opened the door, the long broom stick came at her. She screamed and pulled the door shut again, or at least she tried to. The broomstick was wiggling between the door and the jam.

"This is very unsettling," the man said disdainfully as he motioned for her to step aside. He opened the door and instead of attacking, the broom pulled away sharply. It even seemed to be shuddering. "See here, that is not the behavior I expect! And I will have no more of it," he admonished the cleaning apparatus and its cohorts. "Return to your closet and stay there until you are summoned! Go on, go!"

In disbelief, Nora watched as the broom, the mop, and

all the other instruments used in the attack retreated rather sulkily. "It's not possible," she said as she collapsed to her knees.

"Well, of course it is," argued Robyn as he pulled her back to her feet. "Now, let us go in and make some sense of this *mess* your aunt left behind." He ushered her into the house, but Nora was more than reluctant. He escorted her into the parlor and led her toward the chair that was closest to the hearth. "When was the last time you had any contact with your aunt?"

"You know that Winnie was my aunt?" Nora questioned the odd man and taking her seat.

"Of course…well, she was your great aunt, to be precise. Sister to your grandfather." Robyn nodded. "I knew a great deal about Winnie, and from her I have learned a great deal about you as well over the years."

Feeling odd and out of place abruptly, Nora cowered in the chair. "How did you know Winnie? I never met you here, or heard her talk about you."

"I was her *guide*," he answered, as if discussing the weather. "It was very satisfying, and I so looked forward to being yours as well."

"Her guide," Nora repeated. "Guide to what?"

"She didn't tell you anything, did she?" Frustrated and perturbed, he took a seat across from her. "Not anything?"

Feeling cornered and on the spot, Nora asked, "About what?" Her voice sounded small and fragile. She pulled her feet up into the chair and tucked up into a protective ball. She feared she had lost her mind, but the pain from where he'd pinched her convinced her that something was happening here. And there was the growing lump on her head, convincing her that the broom had stuck her. Impossible as that was, it was also irrefutable.

Robyn shook his head. "I've never heard of such a thing, not telling an initiate.... How could she have trained you if you don't know?"

"Trained me?" Nora felt like a myna bird, repeating what it heard.

Before Nora could ask another question or hear the answer to the last one posed, a rapid tapping sounded at the cottage door. Robyn stood. "You'd best allow me to answer this." He took a deep breath and reluctantly approached the door. "We're expecting another," he informed the girl. "And he's not going to be happy.... Best let me deal with him." Nora wasn't happy with him being there, and the idea of another unwelcome uninvited guest filled her with rage.

"What do you mean another?" But the man in blues, greens, and golds ignored her.

Robyn opened the door and a dark figure stood on the porch. "Liam," he said in a voice that was filled with regret and guilt. "We've a problem...."

Liam pushed past the man, and when Nora glanced toward the foyer, she was a bit shocked to see a man in what appeared to be gypsy apparel. He was taller than Robyn and much more muscular, with dark hair and eyes and swarthy skin. He walked with authority and forceful energy, unlike Robyn, who sort of moved like a gazelle. He turned his dark gaze on Nora cowering in the wingback chair. "Rise and face me!" he demanded.

"I don't think so," Nora said before turning to look away

and pulling up into a ball on the chair.

Liam turned to the other man. "She just refused to face me."

"I'm aware."

"No." Liam shook his head as he marched into the parlor. "No, no, no. You are not allowed to refuse me! It has never been done." He placed himself where the girl had to look at him. "The challenger comes, we duel, you prove your powers...."

"Powers?" She stared at the man. "What powers?"

"She doesn't know," Robyn announced icily.

"Does not know?" Liam repeated, still staring at the girl. "How can this be?"

"Winnie, for some reason, never told her," the man in blue tried to explain.

"Impossible," Liam exclaimed. "How could she train this one if she didn't know?"

"I don't think she did," Robyn confessed.

Liam backed away. "Didn't train her?" His voice went up several octaves.

Robyn shook his head.

"Didn't tell her *anything*?"

Again, the other shook his head.

"She knows *nothing*?" Now the tall, dark stranger, wearing a linen peasant shirt and loose fitted brown trousers tucked into knee boots, collapsed into a chair. "How is that possible?" he demanded, his accent getting thicker as his anger rose.

"I don't know. I arrived only a short time before you did," Robyn stated. "I should have been here weeks ago.

Everything in this transition is...lopsided. She wasn't even expecting me!"

Running his hands through his wild riot of dark waves and curls, Liam's face showed stirrings of anger and confusion. "There has to be a reason," he blurted out. He looked at the young woman curled up in a ball in the chair. "You are Winnie's heir, are you not?"

"Yes," she answered in a weak whisper. "One of them."

Liam leaned forward. "You are the girl she left all this too?"

Nora nodded.

"But she said nothing? She didn't tell you to expect us?"

Nora shook her head. "Not a word."

"Impossible," Liam said darkly. "The Guardian would never do that!" He looked over at Robyn. "Didn't you keep track of the progress of the initiate?"

"That's not what we do," Robyn answered indignantly. "We don't go poking our noses into the training. That's up to the Guardian in residence, as you well know." He too was now in the parlor and standing over the girl. "Our problem is Winnie, and what she didn't do and why." He began to tap his toe of his booted foot impatiently. "When I arrived, this one was being attacked by the broom and mop."

A momentary expression of amusement passed over Liam's features. "Really?"

Nora stirred. "I imagined that," she said defensively. "It didn't happen...brooms and mops don't attack people."

"Ordinarily no," Liam agreed, still amused. "But you and your broom are not ordinary."

Nora glared at him. "It's not my broom, it's Winnie's."

He leaned back and turned to look at the other man. "Robyn, you knew Winnie…I didn't have as much contact. Wouldn't she have left a clue as to why she inconvenienced us?"

"She inconvenienced you?" Nora blinked. "I don't see how—"

"Little one," Liam warned darkly. "Be still for now. Allow us to try and reason this out before we have to deal with *you*." A thin malicious looking smile formed on his handsome lips. "Or would you like us to call out the broom?"

Nora curled tighter. "No, no."

Robyn frowned. "That's really not fair," he accused the man. "It's like teasing a mouse with a cat."

"Effective," Liam stated as he stood up. "You knew Winnie; her testing was long before I was born. So it falls to you, my fine elf, to find the clues so we can sort this out."

The man just called elf nodded. "I agree. She must have left something for us…some trail to follow." He turned to Nora. "You were here when she passed…."

"No, I wasn't," Nora interrupted. Both men stared at her. "I lived in a little town about twelve miles east and north of here until *today*. Aunt Winnie lived here alone, with a nurse at the end."

"A nurse?" Robyn made a sour face. "You were not here to attend her in her hour of death?"

"No, I wasn't," Nora said. This man was making her defensive. "I just told you that."

Liam shook his head. "What's this world coming to?" His Scots Celtic accent deepened as he became disgusted. "What's happened to this family? Don't the Belfry take care of their own here?"

"Winnie didn't ask for any of us. I'd have been here... she told me on May Day that she was going to be busy with the trustees," Nora said, unraveling herself and extending her legs until they reached the floor. "I offered to take my vacation; that is, when I thought I was going to have a vacation...." Nora didn't appreciate the condescending way the dark stranger was treating her. "Winnie said there'd be plenty of time for us to spend together, and I believed her." Her voice trembled when she said the last sentence. She had believed her, had wanted desperately to believe there was still time.

Robyn exhaled in exasperation. "Winnie, I suspect, didn't tell them, any of them, that she was dying. How foolish of the woman." Shaking his head, he began to mutter more to himself than to any of the others in the room as he began to aimlessly pace. "Where would one put down thoughts and secrets?"

"Her journal?" Nora offered. "Winnie once told me that she kept journals, one for each year of her life since she moved in here," Nora informed the two men. "She was always writing things down. I remember asking her when I was about twelve what she was doing, and she said she was baring her soul for future examination. That was the summer she started me keeping a journal when I was here."

"A book of shadows, in volume," Liam said, snapping his fingers loudly. "Young lady, would you recognize these journals?"

Nora glared at him. "Don't be snapping your fingers at me like I'm some trick dog that you can order about," she retorted stubbornly. "I don't think I want you looking at

Winnie's journals." She added, "I don't like you!"

"Like it or not," Liam said. "I'm going to see them."

Suddenly Nora's eyes narrowed, her lips thinned, and she growled back, "Don't bet on it, Bucko!" Standing up for herself against Connie had felt good; this felt glorious!

Chapter 4

Robyn gasped, astounded that the meek and mild creature had taken such a stance. Liam smiled icily, amused and pleased. "So," he crooned darkly. "There is fire beneath that calm. A lioness within the mouse. Good!" He pulled her to her feet. "You're going to need all that fire and ice, Guardian."

Trying to jerk her arm back from the grip that had hauled her out of the comfort and safety of the chair, Nora glowered, "Keep your paws off! And quit calling me that! I'm not this Guardian you keep saying I am!"

Throwing his head back, Liam laughed. Nora wondered fleetingly why it was she could be furious with the man and yet find his laugh so…intriguing.

Robyn tried to move between the two. "I must insist that we conduct ourselves within the usual social rules," he complained. "Kindly unhand her!"

Liam ignored the pleadings of both the elf and Nora. "You want me to go away?" He asked her brutally, and when she nodded he said, "Then show me the journals." His lips curled as he spoke. "The sooner we know why you're not trained, the quicker I'll go. Now, the journals."

"Please," the other asked gently, trying once more for civility.

Nora heard Robyn but didn't acknowledge him. Her eyes were glued to those of the dark Celt. "Fine," she said at last. "Her journals are all kept in the study." She motioned to the alcove. "She wrote in them everyday down here."

"Show me," Liam commanded, releasing the wrist in his grasp.

Nora wondered why she wasn't taking this opportunity to escape. But then, where would she go? This was her home, even if she was suddenly feeling like the outsider here. She walked over to the little room that had been added years ago to give Winnie a nice cheery place to sit and write and watch her beloved wild creatures. What had once been a sun porch had been enclosed. Nora's father had helped design the space when he was young; it contained a built in writing table, good lighting, and a long span of bookshelves that were easy to reach from the confines of a wheelchair. An entire shelf on one wall had been devoted to her journals that she kept, in a year by year order. Nora's fingers went over the leather bindings, and when she reached the current year she pulled it gently from the rest. "This is the one that she was working on this past year. It ends shortly after May Day."

"That's not a book of shadows, or even a grimoire," argued Robyn, who was standing behind Liam.

"Not everything a mage uses is put into the shadows," Liam said prudently. "If you wish to hide something—"

"Leave it in plain sight," Nora finished. She handed the book to the dark Celt. His words and his facial expression had changed her mind about him, if only a bit. She still didn't like him, but she was willing to take a chance on him.

Grinning, Liam nodded and opened the book. Something fell out and dropped to the floor. Liam bent down to look at it. "A ring." He handed the band of metal to Nora. There were a few loose items in the front of the book, and he began to inspect them. "Feathers from an owl," he said, handing the few fluffy objects on a loose piece of parchment to Nora.

"These must have been from old Archimedes," she told him. "That's what Aunt Winnie called the barn owl that took up residence here in the loft over the garage." She touched the feathers gently. They were soft, but a sad reminder that Winnie and her owl friend were no more.

He lifted the parchment, unfolded it carefully, and nodded. "An incantation." He waved the paper at Nora. "Our first clues, little Guardian."

"I can't read that," Nora said. "It looks like gibberish. Does it really say something?"

"It does. It's the language of the rune," he assured her. "But you'll have to take my word for it. Now tell me, where is Winnie buried? We'll need a quick trip to the cemetery tonight."

"She'd not in a cemetery," Nora said, blinking. "She wanted to be cremated; her ashes sit on the mantle." She motioned back toward the room they had exited.

"Barbaric!" interjected Robyn.

"No, very smart," Liam countered. "She must have known we'd be here…and she left these clues." He snorted.

"What better place to have the incantation read than in the privacy of her own parlor?" Reaching for Nora's hand, he said, "Come, it's time to find out why you know nothing of your true inheritance." The harshness had left his voice, and it was now encouraging.

Still holding the ring and the feathers in cupped hands, she walked at the side of the Celt back to the parlor. Liam directed her to stand before the sculpted urn once she'd told him that was Winnie's resting place. He then told her to slip the ring on her finger, but didn't tell her which one. Something inside told her it was for her index finger of her right hand; there was a vague memory of Winnie wearing a ring there. Something Winnie had said about inheriting the ring, that it had been passed down the family line. Now it was Nora's and it felt right. Liam then told her to extend her left hand with the pair of owl feathers toward the urn, and repeat after him the words that were written on the parchment.

Nora looked at him a bit shakily. "Yeah sure, anything you say...this is all a fabrication of my own making. I'm really lying out on the kitchen floor having had something collapse on me when I opened the broom closet," she muttered as she extended her hand with the feathers. "This is all an elaborate hallucination."

Liam snorted, "Just do as I tell you and stop editorializing."

Nora sighed. "Ready when you are, Svengali."

~*~

Liam's expression conveyed he had his doubts as to the accuracy of that statement, but he didn't wish to waste time on arguing or correcting her. *"Ddraig o fywyd; Gwrando fy ple; Gadewch i fy anwylyd siarad â fi."* He read the words from the page.

Nora blinked and turned to look at him, lowering the feathers. "You're kidding," she said.

"*Ddraig o fywyd; Gwrando fy ple; Gadewch i fy anwylyd siarad â fi,*" he repeated insistently.

"Sounds like gobbledygook to me," Nora muttered as she raised her hand with the feathers. "I'm so gonna see a good shrink when I wake up." He repeated the phrase once more, and she echoed his words. "*Ddraig o fywyd; Gwrando fy ple; Gadewch i fy anwylyd siarad â fi.*" Liam was surprised that she was able to mimic him so well.

"Turn around and face the urn again," Liam commanded, a bit impatient that the girl knew so little.

When she'd completed the task, he had her repeat the entire routine again, and then a third time. Nora turned to look at him when she'd finished. "What now?" she asked, sounding a bit ridiculous. Liam wasn't looking at her, but rather at the sculpted urn on the mantel as it began to rock to and fro. It vibrated, and Nora turned to look at it as well. He saw her mouth dropping open.

The lidded top of the sculpture came off with a loud popping sound. Swirls of gray matter arose from the urn and danced in the air. They shimmered like dew drops in the early morning light as they descended like a waterfall in front of the fireplace. A familiar form started to take shape. Nora gasped and collapsed with one word uttered. "Winnie...."

Liam had been standing close enough that he prevented her from being injured as she fainted away. He looked up at the apparition they had called forth. "You have some explaining to do, Guardian," he snapped waspishly.

"I don't have much time," she warned sharply. "Once she wakes I will fade."

"Why didn't you tell her who she is?" Robyn demanded.

"Or train her properly?" Liam shouted at the spirit before them.

"Because I lost the right to do so," the female apparition answered with a shamed face. "Long before Nora was born, when I was a young and foolish Guardian, I made the mistake of making a very foolish and overconfident error. I was young and oh so full of myself," she explained. "It was Samhain, an unusually warm Samhain. I'd had too much mead, I was dancing in the grove…skyclad…and…." She paused, looking a bit embarrassed. "I forgot what a trickster our foe can be."

Robyn struggled for breath. "You danced in the grove with that…*thing*?" Liam saw Robyn shudder and heard the revulsion in his voice. He found himself agreeing with the elf.

Winnie's image nodded. "He tricked me, and the payment I had to render was that I could not properly train my replacement." The ghost looked toward the unconscious young woman. "Years later, when Nora was born, I knew she was the one to take my place, but my hands were already tied."

"You never told her of the lineage?" Robyn asked.

"No."

"She knows nothing?" Liam gazed at the ghost. "Not anything?"

"She's more or less a blank page," Winnie admitted. "And you two have until Samhain to make her a Guardian or…else. I thought I had more time, that I would be here for Samhain, and then go…but I was wrong." Her voice filled with regret. "The future depends on you making sure **It** does not get free. To do that, you must help Nora become a full Guardian. Blank as she may be, she has raw potential, and she has the power it takes to be a Guardian. Though you may not see it, you must help her find it." Both men looked at the girl who was still unconscious. "Whatever you do, you must do it quickly. There must be a Guardian by Samhain!" The apparition began to fade. "She awakens, Blessed Be...."

~*~

Nora moaned and opened her eyes, looked up into Liam's dark eyes, and yelped. She cowered and backed away, hitting the shoes of the other man, and screamed again. "Oh God! It wasn't a dream...you're both really here!"

Liam chuckled, ignoring the exasperated comment muttered by Robyn. "And you are really here as well," he informed the cowering girl. "So let us formally introduce ourselves." He was kneeling beside her, offered his hand, saying, "I am Liam Belfry, and I am the Chovihano of the Fillip, the shaman of the People of the Horse in the land of the heather." He spoke with pride and conviction. "And I've come a long way to be of service to you, little cousin." This last part was said with more kindness than Nora could remember from others she called cousin. Certainly Connie had never sounded this kind to her, and she had been raised with her.

"I'm sure that's very nice." Nora stared at the hand extended her way, refusing to take it when his statement a few moments before struck her. "Wait. What did you say? You're a Belfry? We're related? How is that possible?"

Liam shrugged. "It is what it is," he said with a wry smile. "As the current chovihano, it is my duty and honor to come and test the mettle of the new Guardian. It has been our line's honor for nearly a thousand years. Guardians come and go, and all need to be tested. Who better to test the Belfry Guardian than the Belfry Chovihano?"

"Right," she said, still pulling away. She was no longer worried that she'd lost her mind so much as she had landed in the middle of a nightmare.

"She doesn't believe you," Robyn said sarcastically as he crossed his arms and glared at the pair on the floor. "She thinks we are escapees from some lunatic asylum." Nora wondered if he was reading her mind, and she didn't like the invasion of what she considered her privacy.

Liam cocked one brow, read the girl's body language, and frowned. "I'm a chovihano, and he's an elf. And you, my reluctant little mouse, are the last in a great line of Belfry Guardians."

Nora closed her eyes, laid back down, and chanted, "I'm asleep, I'm asleep, I'm asleep…."

Robyn picked up the cap from the mantel and replaced it on the urn, "How could she expect us to train this thing into a Guardian in eight weeks?" He shook his head. "The creature has no knowledge!" He pouted. "It can't be done. We are doomed. The world is going to come to an end."

"She's a Belfry." Liam ignored the elf and studied the girl. "I see fire beneath that calm and mousy exterior. Besides, Winnie said the girl has potential."

Nora opened an eye. "You're still here." It was more statement than question. "Go away."

"No," the man refused. "I came to test you, and test you I will. I'm sworn."

"I don't care if you're the man in the moon," she moaned. "I'm not this…Guardian you keep harping on!"

"Not yet, perhaps," Liam agreed before his voice turned very dark. "But you will be."

Chapter 5

Nora didn't like the sound of that, nor did she like the look on the face of the man in what she'd mistaken as gypsy garb. Something told her this wasn't the kind of man who gave up easily. "I don't even know what this Guardian thing is," she maintained. "And I don't care, I just want you to go away."

Robyn began to pace and mutter angrily in a foreign tongue. Liam motioned for Nora to get up off the floor, and then motioned for her to watch the elf. He seemed very entertained by the antics and the conversation the elf was having. Nora watched, but not with the same amusement. She couldn't understand what the man was muttering, but by the tone it wasn't very complimentary toward her or toward Winnie. Every now and again he would pause and shake a finger at the urn while continuing the dialogue he was having with himself.

"He's upset," Nora whispered to the Celt, who nodded.

"But why at me?" she questioned.

"At the fact of you," the Celtic gypsy shrugged. "More the fact that you don't know anything about anything. Or even who or what you are."

"He's mad at Winnie too," she observed.

"With reason," Liam assured the girl. Pointing to the elf, he said, "He'll go on like this until he's out of wind. That could take some time, and you and I really don't have time to waste, so I suggest we quietly leave him to his tantrum and adjourn to somewhere where I can give you an outline of what we are up against." He motioned toward the alcove. "We'll be close enough that he won't miss us."

Nora nodded, unsure of why she was accepting this suggestion.

Once they were seated in the alcove, Liam asked if she had any question she wanted answered right away. Nora leaned forward. "Am I mad, or did a ghost appear?"

"No, you are not mad, and yes, you saw the spirit of your great aunt."

"That's not possible." Nora shook her head and leaned back. "Ghosts are just stories to scare little kids into behaving."

"Sometimes," the Celt agreed. "But not always."

A loud rant reached them, and Nora winced. "What is a Guardian?" She'd leaned forward, keeping her voice quiet, not wishing for the elf to join them.

"A Guardian," Liam began his explanation, "is a being born of mortal coil, but who has magic at his or her command."

Nora held up a hand. "Wait, a mortal who can use magic...."

"Very adeptly."

Nora laughed. "You're telling me that Winnie could use magic?" Now she'd heard everything. Winnie couldn't even manage to use a cell phone, but she could use magic?

"She was a very powerful witch, even before she became the Guardian," Liam exclaimed.

"Who you calling a witch?" Nora demanded, standing up to defend Winnie's honor.

"Many of the Belfry women have practiced the craft." Liam didn't seem fazed by the outburst. "Her great aunt Harriet before her and her great aunt Agatha before her…just to name a few of *your* heritage. Our family line of witches and wizards goes back to the old kingdoms, when Scotland was known as Alba and Ireland known as Éire. Long before we adopted the name Belfry; which I always thought was rather a funny joke."

Nora's mouth dropped open. "That's a lie."

"Truth is truth," he claimed without sounding smug. "Our people crossed the mists long before they ever dreamed of crossing the oceans. Surely someone told you fairy tales of Mist Walkers when you were in your pram."

"Mist Walkers." Nora blinked, her green eyes growing large. "You're saying that Winnie was a witch…but witches are bad and do evil things…and…and…," Nora sputtered. "And Winnie was good!"

"Papist propaganda," he chuckled. "I won't say all witches are good, but not all are bad. You must learn that for yourself, as you discover who and what you are, Nora Belfry."

"I'm nothing," Nora said, shrinking back a bit. "Just a girl whose great aunt took pity and left her some property and money. Who without it would be a homeless, jobless…

failure."

"How does one born to the Belfry name become so timid and faint-hearted?" he asked harshly. "I have seen fire in you! I have seen you roar! You won't convince me now it does not exist."

"I doubt anyone else would agree with you," Nora mused. "Up until a few days ago I was living pretty much from one day to the next…working in the same bookstore that I worked in when I was in high school. Living above it in a studio apartment that isn't as big as my aunt Winnie's kitchen. I am a little nobody from a little nobody town, I've never managed anything or been anywhere…. If you're expecting a Belfry with fire, you should be appearing to my cousin Connie; she's got fire enough for a dragon." She sank in the chair dejectedly.

"This Connie is a Belfry?" Liam asked.

"Her mother was; Connie's last name is Logan."

Holding up a hand, Liam stopped her from continuing. "The Belfry Witch is Belfry born," he informed her. "But who said you are nothing?"

"Connie," Nora sighed.

"And you believed her?"

Nora shrugged. "Connie is older, smarter, faster, prettier…. Yeah, I believe her, and so does everyone else who matters." Nora stood up and stepped between the space of Liam's chair and her own. "Connie's dad was a high powered go getter; her mother is my dad's older sister. My dad is the youngest son of Aunt Winnie's brother. My Uncle John, the oldest brother, runs the family business, and my dad worked for him until he became ill. Because of the stocks and bonds he'd accumulated, he was able to afford to pack it in and leave while I was in college. I got the studio apartment while I was in school; it was easy to pay for it on the salary I earned. I didn't go to a fancy finishing school like Connie did, or to a big ten college. I went to the local community college, and only lived in a dorm my first year. She has a masters in business, and I only have a bachelors in language." Her voice sounded doleful and glum. "Connie's dad could afford to send her and David to big name schools, where they lived in dorms and came home only for holidays."

"Go on," Liam urged. Nora hesitated, but then the story poured out of her.

"My dad had good medical coverage with the family company, but even so, his heart surgeries ate into what he and my mom had set aside originally for my education," Nora explained. "His first operation was when I was twelve. I don't think Connie knew about it, or maybe she didn't care. It didn't affect her personally." She glanced about the room. "I came here that summer so that my mother could spend her time tending to Daddy. Winnie made sure I had wonderful memories to look back on." She frowned. "I thought all of us had wonderful memories of that summer. We were here together, Connie, David, and me." A chill moved through her as she remembered Connie's harsh words in the lawyer's office. "Turns out, I'm the only one who had a good time. Connie hated the summer vacations here with Aunt Winnie, and when she found out that I was the one to whom she'd left this place, she tried to force me to sign it over to her to sell."

Hearing steel come into her voice, Liam smiled. "And you refused."

"I couldn't sell this place," Nora said firmly. "I loved it

here…and I loved being with Winnie. Going up and down the moraines, learning the names of the birds and the plants and catching tadpoles…."

"Wait." Liam stood up. "You did what?"

"What…that Winnie taught us the names of the plants and animals in the forest?" Nora answered in a questioning tone.

A wide smile spread on the face of the handsome gypsy, making him seem a bit less intimidating and friendlier. "That sly old witch," he mused. "She found herself a loophole."

"Loophole?" Nora asked.

Liam stood up. "You are not a nothing, little cousin," he assured her. "You learned these lessons that your aunt taught you?" She nodded. "And you fought with this strong willed older cousin?" She nodded again. "And you rebelliously came here to live?"

"I had nowhere else to go," she confessed. "My folks live six states away. I'd be damned before I'd go crawling to Uncle John to ask for help. Hell, he and Jack didn't even have the decency to come to the reading of Winnie's will. Too busy running the business." Nora felt the surge of resentment toward the Belfry business rise again. She had blamed the family business for her father's illness, and his brother for her parents needing to leave this climate. More, she blamed Uncle John for them leaving her.

"Ha!" The Celt howled. "There is fire in you."

"Foolish pride is not *fire*," Nora argued.

Liam rose to his feet, approached her slowly, and stood gazing down into her widened eyes. "There is fire in you, little Belfry Witch," he assured her. "I have seen it, I have heard it. I will be damned if I'm going to let you or anyone else waste it." One hand moved gently toward her cheek. "Do not be fooled by outer beauty. This Connie may be all flash and flicker, and may talk a good game, but does she have the devotion that you have? Does she treasure the hours spent here learning the names of the flora and fauna?"

"No," Nora answered, quite certain that Connie didn't even remember what they had learned as kids. "She said she hated this place."

"This Connie is not the Guardian." Liam stroked her cheek. "If she were, Winnie would have left everything to her. She's not even a Belfry at heart, she's a Logan."

"I thought Winnie was just being kind because I came to visit when everyone else was too busy," Nora confessed. "This place is out of the way, and they all have important jobs. I was never too busy, and I so loved being here with Winnie."

"No job is more important than that of the Guardian, but it is also the least likely to win awards or even be appreciated," Liam warned. "For few in the mortal realm know who the Guardians are or what they do. They keep the balance without ever looking for compensation or accolades; they are the silent sentinels who keep the darkness at bay."

His hand on her skin felt warm and comforting, and Nora was forgetting that he was a stranger. Something in his touch seemed as familiar as sunshine. "How?"

"By magic," he teased gently.

"But I don't know any magic," Nora warned timidly.

"You do. It's as much a part of you as breathing, you just don't know it yet," he assured her. "And you will know how to use it, when you really need it." His smile made her feel warm, in a way no other man had ever made her feel. Nora blushed, her skin warming under his touch. "You are going to have to trust me, little Belfry cousin."

"Nora," she said shyly.

"Nora," he repeated, and then looked toward the room where the elf was still carrying on a one way argument. "We'd better get him on track," he said teasingly. "Or he'll stand there arguing with that urn for hours." He removed his hand from her cheek. "Come, Nora." He offered the hand that had tenderly stroked her cheek to her.

"All right." She placed her hand in his.

Robyn was argued out, and was butting his forehead on the mantel. "We're doomed," he moaned. "Utterly doomed."

"Not utterly," Liam disagreed, placing Nora before him and resting hands on her shoulders. "Not as long as we've a willing candidate."

"She knows nothing," Robyn contended, his forehead still on the mantel.

"She knows more than she thinks she knows," Liam countered. "We have but to unleash the harness that holds her back."

Turning his head and giving the pair a disparaging look, Robyn grumbled, "How old are you?"

"Twenty-eight," Nora answered with a blush.

"At twenty-eight she should have full command of her powers; she should be in her prime!" Robyn said, turning back to butt his head on the mantle again. "You expect me to train her to be a Guardian in eight weeks?" He laughed cruelly. "It's impossible, it's never been done."

Nora looked back at the Celt, whose hands were still firmly on her shoulders. "Is he right?"

Liam shook his head. "Robyn, just because something has never been done does not make it impossible."

The elf paused in mid thud. "Well, that's…true." He looked up at the urn. "But we're years behind. Winnie was Harriet's apprentice from the time she was sixteen until Harriet passed away, when Winnie was twenty-five and took up the title." He approached the young woman. "Still, she is a Belfry…and she's Winnie's heir…." He looked like a man trying to argue himself into something he really didn't want to do. "There has to be a spark of magic in there, or why else would Winnie leave the title to her?" He moved closer and looked deeply into the eyes staring at him. "Is there magic in there?" he asked aloud as he stared. Suddenly he pulled back, looked at the Celtic shaman, and nodded. "There's still a chance; slim, but a chance."

"Welcome to the next stage of your life, Nora Belfry, soon to be the Guardian of Misty Hollow," Liam crooned as he handed the girl over to the elf. "Teach her well, for in eight weeks…all hell breaks loose."

Nora gasped. "Hold it, nobody said anything about hell breaking loose!"

Chapter 6

Four weeks passed, one day dragging itself into another. Nora felt she was no closer to being able to use even the simplest of spells that Robyn was trying relentlessly to teach her. From sunrise to sundown, she was drilled on incantations and runes and potions. Each night she cried herself to sleep, wondering if the madness would ever end.

She rose on the morning a month after she'd moved in and went to the kitchen, avoiding the broom closet. Its tedious inhabitants were no closer to accepting her as the title-holder or rightful property owner. Whenever she had to come into the kitchen without the protection of Robyn or Liam in her company, it was risky. It seemed every stick of furniture in the cottage held an opinion, and a good many seemed against her. This morning she tiptoed into the kitchen to put on a kettle of water to make some herbal tea. She'd given up coffee, as it seemed to make her too jittery while she was trying to learn whatever it was Robyn would be teaching. She was moving slowly past the closet on her way to the pantry for the tea canister when the closet door flew open and the broom shot out, seeking to maim her.

After weeks of being attacked, her instincts and her reflexes seemed to have sharpened. This time she didn't cower, or dash out of the room, or run calling out to her two male companions. This time she reached out, grabbed the offending implement, and growled at it in a very terse manner. "You're headed to kindling!" The broom stopped in mid-attack and went still.

Nora returned it to the closet without much thought. It was still dark out, and her head was fuzzy from dreams. Once the attacker had been returned to its clip, Nora went back about her business of getting a cup of tea made. Sitting quietly in the dimness of the early morning, dressed in her robe and slippers, she cupped her hands about the steaming mug that contained the brew.

"Why can't I just say the words in English?" she muttered into the cup. "Why does it have to be Old Welsh or Old Latin; what's so great about them? They are dead languages." Much like Robyn, she'd taken to arguing and discussing things aloud to herself. "I don't see what difference it makes. This should be easier." Her face over the cup, she breathed in the fragrance and bouquet of the brewed herbs. "Herbs and steam," she muttered tranquilly. "Clear my dreams…." She sipped the brew and blinked.

Placing the mug down, she shook her head. It couldn't be that simple, she told herself. Could it?

Liam found her seated in the breakfast nook with a now cold cup of tea before her. "How long have you been up?"

"Hours," she answered, not taking her gaze off the mug before her.

He stared at the cup as he came near. "You've hardly touched that…it's gone cold."

"It wasn't before."

Shrugging, he moved across the room to heat up the water again. In the weeks since he and Robyn had been residing with her, they had both learned to use the kitchen's conveniences. He returned to sit across from her while his tea was steeping. Only then did he become aware of her attire, or the fact that her hair was down and loose. "You look different," he remarked.

"Do I?" Her eyes opened wider.

He nodded. "You should wear your hair down more often," he said. "It's becoming, and flatters you."

Too vexed over other matters, Nora didn't give a thought to her appearance. "Liam," she addressed him respectfully. "Why do incantations have to be spoken in Latin or in Welsh?"

He shrugged. "I'm not sure," he answered. "I think it has something to do with family roots. I use the Gaelic Rom tongue when I cast or chant, because my line's roots are Celtic gypsy. I suppose if I really wanted to I could cast in Scots Gaelic."

"But Liam, I don't think of myself as an Old World Celt…I think of myself as *American*," she murmured, trying to sound logical. "Welsh, Latin, and Gaelic are foreign to me."

He sipped his tea and glanced over at her. "Yes. But—"

"Liam," Nora made a case. "Winnie was the last link to the old world and the old ways. She went overseas with her Aunt Harriet and did the continent before she was a debutante. I've never even been out of the continental U.S.A." She leaned back against the wooden bench. "So why Welsh or Gaelic? Why Latin?"

He shrugged. "Tradition."

"But Liam," she questioned. "I'm not a traditional witch, not even close. If I were I'd be able to do things. I can't even do simple levitation." She shook her head. "Robyn says I should be able to use simple transference of energy; I should be able to use kinetics at this point."

Her distant cousin set down his cup and listened.

"What if we're doing this all wrong?" she asked.

"All wrong?" His jaw tightened.

Nora stood up, carried her cup to the sink, and poured the rest of her untouched tea down the drain. "What if it's the way I'm being forced to use something I'm not used to… something that feels much too foreign to me? Didn't you say this is supposed to feel natural?" She placed the mug in the sink. "What if the words are in the wrong tongue?"

"Did something happen down here?" he asked.

Still at the sink, Nora looked at the door of the broom closet. "The broom attacked like it always does when I'm alone, but this time…." She took a deep breath. "It stopped when I threatened it."

Liam smiled. "You threatened the broom?" The smile widened, and he chuckled.

She nodded, "Yes, I did. I told it that it was headed to kindling, and it stopped."

He covered his growing smile. "That's progress."

"That's not all," she continued. "I was muttering to myself, and said something clever over my steaming tea, and the fogginess I'd awakened with abated."

This had his attention. "What did you say?"

"Herbs and steam," she repeated the phrase, "clear my dreams."

Liam tapped long fingers to his chin. "Rudimentary, and primitive," he judged. "But most definitely well on the way to being a full incantation. Very clever, Nora, very clever indeed."

"But Liam, I said it in English," she said emphatically. "Not in Gaelic, not in Latin, not in Greek! I said it in English, and it felt natural."

"Your argument has merit," Liam admitted. "But I don't think Robyn will agree…he's a bit stubborn, and extremely traditional. He doesn't approve of change." He looked about the room, looking for some simple task she could try. "Move that envelope."

"Where?"

"That one." He pointed across the counter.

"Where to?" she asked more directly.

Liam laughed. "Such confidence," he teased. "Move it out of the holder and down to the counter."

Focusing, Nora took a deep breath. "Envelope move to my will." The paper in the bill holder shook violently, but remained held tight.

"I think you may be onto something," Liam said as he stood up and moved across the room. "Try again. This time, try to make your words rhyme."

Nora frowned. "Rhyme?"

"Just do it. If only to humor me."

She shrugged. "Envelope isn't an easy word to rhyme…." She cleared her mind, took a deep breath, and chanted,

"Envelope there across from me, fall out and do be free."

Liam winced at the inadequate rhyme, but watched as the paper inched out of the holder. "You need to work on your word flow and rhythm," he suggested. "But this is progress."

"Progress," she shot back. "I barely made it an inch out of the holder." She wiped the beads of sweat gathering on her brow with her hand. "I'm sweating bullets here, and you call that progress." She crossed her arms on the table and laid her head on her folded appendages.

Liam nodded happily. "The point is you made it move. Four weeks ago it wouldn't have even vibrated."

"Big deal," she moaned.

"Baby steps, little cousin," he offered, with a supportive pat to her shoulder. "But they are steps."

"I feel drained," she moaned.

"You are new to this," he said.

Looking up off her arms, she frowned. "It shouldn't be this hard, not if I'm born to this as you insist that I am."

"If you'd been training since you were twelve this would have been a snap. You'll grow stronger," he said with confidence. "Only trouble is, we have to convince Robyn to work with us. Not keep to the old path."

Her head went back on her arms. "You know what he'll say," she muttered. "He'll say, 'We have to stay to the way it's always been done. That tradition is sacred.' That *he* knows best how to guide a Guardian." At the end she was mimicking the elf.

"I'll convince him otherwise," Liam offered generously. "But you don't look so well."

"That vegan elf has 'purged' all the animal products out

of me," she moaned before once more trying to raise her head to look at him. "I need meat." She groaned. "I'm so hungry I could eat a cow…fresh butchered! Those birds out on the patio are starting to look appetizing."

"If you could eat anything right now, what would it be?"

"Bacon and eggs," she said, descending onto her arms. "With cheese toast and fried potatoes."

"Do we have any of those ingredients?"

She looked up. "Yes."

"Well, the elf isn't up yet," he said in a conspiratorial manner. Pulling the weak girl to her feet, he pushed her toward the stove. "Just tell me what you need, and I'll bring it to you."

Forty minutes later Robyn entered the kitchen, making a face at the odors in the air that greeted him. "What is that stench?"

"Breakfast," Nora growled back, waving a sausage at him. "And if you ever try and take meat out of my diet again, I'll take a bite out of you, Elf-boy!"

Liam laughed heartily, and Nora gave him a wink. It felt good to have Liam on her side, even if it was just for this occasion.

Robyn glowered back. "This is the thanks I get for trying to unpollute your system?"

"Get this," she said, rising up like a banshee. "I am not an herbivore…I have teeth to tear meat, and I happen to like the flavor." She felt power surge as she spoke. "I am not an elf! I need the proteins that are given in eating meat!"

"It's barbaric," Robyn whined.

"Then don't watch," she stated without remorse. "But I'm

going to eat meat, and lots of it."

"Talk to her," Robyn implored the Celt.

"I think she's right," Liam defended the girl. "And she may have found the reason she's not responding and excelling." He waited until the elf turned his full attention to him. "We're using the wrong language."

"The wrong language?" the elf inquired. Nora watched his expression go from repulsed by the eating of animal flesh, to one of indignity at such a suggestion.

"You've been trying to teach her incantations and potions in the old Gaelic language, but that's not her native tongue," Liam pointed out.

"Old Gaelic and old Latin are the norm," Robyn insisted in his stubborn reasoning, his jaw clenched tightly.

"For whom?"

Robyn crossed his arms, shifted his stance, and dug in. "It is the tradition of the Belfry Guardian."

"I see." Liam lifted his coffee mug. "Robyn, in what language do you converse at home?"

"Gelven Elven," he answered, decidedly vexed. "You know that."

"And when you come across the mists?"

"Anglo speak."

"And you've been doing this for how long?"

Robyn narrowed his gaze. "Do you have a point?"

"Robyn, you and I are used to dealing with a fully trained Guardian, someone who has a working use of the Gaelic and Latin." He smiled across at the young woman who was looking much revived. "Nora does not have a working use of any of that. She isn't comfortable with it; it's a foreign tongue."

"She's being lazy," Robyn accused.

Nora dropped her fork, turned, and glared. "I so wish a wet dish towel would smack you!"

Quick as lightning, the damp towel that was sitting on the counter flew across the room and pelted the elf, who was taken by as much surprise as the girl who had uttered the words.

"You did that," he accused Liam.

"I did not," Liam proclaimed. "She did." He pointed to Nora. "And she said the commands in *English*."

"She's an American," Robyn countered. "She doesn't even speak proper English!" Holding the damp towel that was still trying to strike away, Robyn looked at Nora. "It's unorthodox," he nitpicked. "But we'll give it a try. However, if you fail, we go back to Gaelic! Now kindly tell this towel to let up! This is an undignified way to treat your guide."

Nora smiled. "He's learned his lesson, towel, you can stop, for now." It dropped to the floor and remained still. She smiled at the elf; hopefully he'd caught the intended threat at the end of her statement.

Robyn refused to take a seat with the pair at the table; he said he couldn't bear the stench of animal flesh any longer. He picked up a plate, filled it with vegan food, and marched out to the patio.

Liam beamed a smile as he finished his meal. "You're a much better cook than the elf," he praised.

Nora lingered over her cup of tea. "I feel like I just swam an ocean," she confessed to her co-conspirator.

Liam smiled. "Baby steps."

Chapter 7

Still drained from the little progress she'd unexpectedly made, Nora begged off from the morning schedule in favor of curling up in the overstuffed club chair on the sun porch. She had taken the last of Winnie's journals out there, hoping it would give her a glimmer of what it was her aunt had expected of her. Even if only a hint, Nora would have been elated. For four weeks she'd held a resentment that her aunt's apparition couldn't speak if she were aware. She'd loved Winnie more than anyone ever, and to be denied even that, hurt. She sat in the chair, one of the places that Winnie had loved to sit, and tried to commune with the afterlife, only to be denied. The soft shadows that the autumn leaves cast lured her into a peaceful slumber.

~*~

Liam found her sleeping peacefully in the chair, and motioned for Robyn to follow him out to the back garden. "We'll let her rest," he said soundly. "She's earned it."

~*~

Her dreams were as peaceful as the house. She was safe, warm, and felt a sense of being cared for. A faint scent filled the room. "Winnie," she whispered softly in her sleep, sensing the presence of the elderly woman she loved nearly as much as she loved her parents. The gentle breeze that had leaves dancing before descending left shadows on the floor and throughout the room; even in slumber Nora was aware of movement. The cocoon that held her gently gave way to a dark energy. Nora was dragged from sleep by Connie's strident voice calling her name, and her hand roughly gripping Nora's shoulder.

"Wake up, stupid," her cousin demanded.

Nora opened her eyes reluctantly. "What are you doing here?" she asked. The last person Nora wanted to see standing in her home was Connie. But there she was, looking down at her with those disapproving eyes and that smug expression.

"I had hoped you'd come to your senses." Connie looked perturbed that Nora was slumbering in the middle of the morning. "But here you are, lazing about, not even looking for a new job! How do you expect to pay your bills?"

"I don't think my finances are any of your concern," Nora murmured. She pulled close in, protecting herself.

"Nora," Connie said sharply. "Wake up and smell the coffee." For Nora it was as if she could read Connie's thoughts. Connie had been certain that a few weeks of living out here in the middle of nowhere full time must be irritating, because SHE would find it irritating. "You can't live out here in the sticks! This isn't civilized!"

"Of course I can," Nora disagreed lightly as she rolled to her side. "Now be good enough to go away." She closed her eyes, thinking Connie would take the hint. "I'm taking a nap."

Taking hold of Nora's arm with fingers that were like a vice, Connie yanked her upright. "I'm talking to you; do me the courtesy of paying attention."

Nora remembered that tone; it was Connie's do as I tell you tone. "What do you want?" She hauled herself upright and glared at the other. "I don't recall inviting you over. How did you get in?"

"The front door wasn't even locked! Anyone could walk in! Look at you," Connie barked. "It's nearly noon and you're not even dressed. You're falling apart! You've got no job, no way to support yourself or this…hovel."

"It's not a hovel," Nora interrupted defensively. "It's an Art's and Craft's cottage." With Connie being in real estate, Nora was surprised she wasn't aware of the cottage style. Just because it was old didn't mean it wasn't important.

"You've not talked to anyone in the family since you moved in here."

"How would you know?" Nora demanded. "Just because I don't sit on the phone with you, does not mean I haven't called anyone. I talked to my mother just yesterday. She's fine, by the way."

"She doesn't count," Connie said coldly. "She's not really part of the family."

"Oh? Who does count, Connie? You? David? If my mother doesn't count, then neither does your father." Nora could feel the flames that were building in her brain. "He's not a Belfry, he's a Logan…and so are you." She glared at the intruder.

For a moment Nora thought Connie was going to strike her for the remark. "This house is no good for you," Connie declared. "I can get you top price for it, and we can get you a nice condo downtown, but we need to move now." She fumbled with the briefcase she was carrying.

"I don't want to live downtown."

"Fine, then a nice townhouse in one of the better burbs." Connie acted like she was conceding, making a concession. "Maybe even Kenilworth."

"I don't want to sell the cottage," Nora affirmed loudly. "I *like* living here."

"You won't come winter, when you can't get out of the driveway." Connie made it sound threatening. "Stuck here all alone, no food, no electricity…. No heat!"

"Winnie had an emergency generator hooked up six years ago," Nora informed her cousin tersely. "The pantry is full of canned veggies from the garden. And have you forgotten how many fireplaces this place has?" She pointed toward the outside. "I've got plenty of firewood stacked already. Enough for two winters."

"Stop putting a brave face on it, Nora," Connie taunted. "I know this is not the kind of place a woman of *our generation* would be happy in."

"No Connie, it's not the kind of place that *you'd* be happy with; *I* love it here. I'm not you!" Nora said firmly. "*I* have no desire to sell."

"Stop being so stubborn and stupid," Connie snapped.

"Nora, you're not going to believe what that vegan has done now," a voice called from the kitchen.

Nora saw the accusing look come into Connie's eyes as she demanded, "Who's that?"

Liam came into the parlor carrying a woven basket full

of ripe tomatoes, some of the last of the season's crop. "Oh, I'm sorry, sweetheart. I didn't know you had company." He looked over at Connie.

"Who are you?" Connie demanded hotly.

"Liam." Nora uttered his name in surprise before she could stop herself. She wanted to warn him off, send him back to the safety of the kitchen, but it was too late.

Connie laughed. "What kind of name is that?"

"Scottish," he informed her haughtily. "And you are?" Nora noticed he was giving Connie right back what she had dished out.

"Constance Logan, Nora's cousin."

"Oh." He looked at Nora. "This is she?"

Nora bit back the laughter that nearly choked her as she saw Connie's face color with anger. She nodded. "Yes."

Liam handed the basket of ripe tomatoes to Nora as if Connie didn't matter. "Robyn says *these* are 'worthy' of his efforts to make a halfway decent marinara." He sat on the arm of the chair that Nora was seated in and stroked the hair back from her face. "Oh, and he's out there crooning to the last of the cucumbers. He wants to know if you have good olive oil, or if he's stuck with muck."

Connie glared. "We have family business to discuss," she informed the man before getting harsh. "Tell the Euro-trash to make himself scarce." Connie then turned her back on Liam as if he didn't exist. She glared at Nora, expecting her to obey blindly.

Nora's eyes erupted in bright green fire; Liam saw it and sat still to see how the fledgling handled the situation. Nora's voice shook with anger as she addressed her uninvited guest.

She turned her head slowly in her cousin's direction. "Liam was invited here; were you?"

Connie's lips parted, but no words were spoken. Never had Nora spoken to her in such defiance, and not before strangers.

"You don't have any authority here; this is *my* house, thanks to Aunt Winnie." Nora stood up to Connie. "And I am not selling it. Not to you, and not to your friendly investors!" When Connie's eyes opened wide, Nora laughed. "Did you think I hadn't heard about the people trying to buy up the land that's not deeded to the forest preserve? It's been in all the papers for months, Connie...how they want to build a seasonal resort here. Winnie told them no, and so will I as often as they ask."

"It's top dollar," Connie argued. "You could live anywhere...." She looked over at the man seated on the arm of the chair. "Even keep your Euro playmate."

"A kept man," he mused. "Oh, that's something I've never tried. It might be fun."

"Forgive Connie's rudeness," Nora implored the man. "She's not pleasant when she doesn't get her way."

"We don't need to discuss *family matters* in front of *strangers*," Connie said defensively. "These are things that should be kept quiet...in the family."

"When was the last time you thought of me as family?" inquired Nora. "You never invited me to do anything with you when we were growing up. That is, unless you were forced to. When you had theater tickets you took a total stranger, and then bragged about it right in front of me. You knew I would have loved to see that play. When you planned your Greek vacation, you went with investors. You didn't even inquire if I would like to come along. When you got married, not that it lasted very long, you asked *his second cousin* to witness. You've never invited me to see your home. I wasn't invited to your bridal shower, for that matter. Were you afraid I'd embarrass you, just as you've always embarrassed me? The moment you were old enough to take a job and ditch Winnie and me, you did and you never once looked back. So don't be pulling the 'family' card out; it won't work. You have never thought of me as family." She reached down and picked up the basket of vine ripened tomatoes. "I think we're finished here. Why don't you show yourself out?"

Connie shook her head. "I'm trying to help you; this man is only after the money you're going to come into from the sale of this rat trap." She sneered at Liam. "Not that it's going to be all that much."

"Money is not what *he* wants," Nora argued. "You'd never understand that, would you? To you and David, I'm nothing more than an object in the way of your desires, as always."

"Smarten up, toots," Connie sneered. "A man like that sure doesn't want you for your… charms. He'll be gone as soon as he grows bored, just like Daniel."

"Leave," Nora said coldly.

A colder, even icier than usual smirk came to Connie's lips. "Think about the offer…it won't be long before the investors find enough land and they won't need this dump." She turned on her heels and left.

Liam stood up, turned Nora toward him, and pulled her into his arms. "She's watching from the porch," he warned.

81

"Let's play this up." He tipped her face upward, lowered his lips to hers, and kissed her. Nora's hands clung to his shirt. He ended the kiss only when they heard the quick clip of Connie's heeled shoes leave the porch. "She's gone," he said. "You're right. She's not pleasant."

Nora was still holding tightly to his shirt. "Why did you do that?"

"I wanted to," Liam admitted. "She gave me a good excuse."

"Oh." She blushed. "You didn't have to." She couldn't shrink back as his arms were not about to release her. There was a sense of security, of belonging, of being accepted, and Nora didn't really want that to end.

"Why do you let her make you feel so small, little cousin?" Liam asked gently. "Why do you fear her?"

"While I have the Belfry name," Nora confessed, "I've always known that she had what Grandfather called the Belfry dynamism. I was a bookworm, and she…was the most popular girl in school, as well as a top student. She never had to work at succeeding, it came naturally to her. In Grandfather's eyes, she was tops in the family…and in business, right after cousin Jack, the family namesake." Drawing comfort from his arms, she rested her head on his chest. "Grandfather didn't approve of my father…called Dad a disappointment in front of everyone, and extended that disapproval to me. He said we were weak, and not worthy of the name Belfry."

"And yet, it is you to whom Winnie left the title of Guardian," Liam reminded her. "Can you imagine Connie living in peace with nature? Sacrificing to insure that the portal here is kept safe?" He tipped her face up, gazed into her eyes, and murmured, "Would she risk all that there is to learn in eight weeks what took others half a lifetime to learn? No." He kissed her forehead. "Winnie knew who was true of heart."

"You say that like you believe it," Nora moaned.

"You should believe it too," he assured her, then laughed gently. "Now, we really must go rescue the vegetable garden from that vegan."

Nora chuckled. She was glad that Liam hadn't asked about Daniel. She had a feeling explaining that mess was not going to be easy.

Chapter 8

After dinner, Nora wrapped a shawl about her shoulders and stepped out to the patio. The nights were turning cooler; the leaves had changed from green to flame and gold and red. Many had already fallen, and more would fall in the four weeks left before Samhain. The garden would be bare soon. All but the pumpkins and late fruit on the vines were already harvested. Herbs hung in the rafters of the enclosed back porch, drying. The porch always smelled wonderful in the weeks of herbal drying.

The air was heavy with the fragrance of early autumn, wet loam, early leaves decaying, and the last sweet blossoms. Even the indigenous plants were putting on their best last shows of color. Winnie's night blooming garden was nearly played out, and would soon go dormant. Most of the lilies and creepers were going into hibernation. Listening to the sounds of the forest, Nora tried to forget the visit earlier. A coyote bayed at the moon, and a chill ran up her spine.

Liam found her listening to the mournful sound when he came looking for her. "Sad music, that," he said, coming behind her and placing his hands on her shoulders.

"I've always loved their song," Nora admitted. "Sad and so full of melancholy."

"I think there must be some Celtic gypsy blood in you after all," he teased.

"Mama's side had travelers," she nodded, amused at his left handed compliment. "But it was Winnie who made me love the sounds of the woods at night...or in the daytime, for that matter. I remember the first time I heard a red tailed hawk." Her face lit up from within. "Or heard the cranes when the young hatched...such music."

"Winnie was right to choose you," he whispered in her ear.

Nora was about to turn, hoping he'd kiss her again, when a sound chilled both of them. It wasn't a coyote, a hawk, or a stag. It wasn't human either. "What was that?" she asked, looking up at his worried face.

"That was the first wakening cry of the creature known as Garnel." Liam looked more than concerned about the sound. "In its natural form it can be fearsome. Makes itself look like a man...that is how it entices its human prey."

The creature in the woods howled again. This time, Robyn came flying out the back of the house. "Where's Nora?" he cried out. Seeing her beside the dark Celt, he rushed to her other side and began to drag her back toward the house. "It's not safe out here now, come inside!"

Nora looked for help from Liam. He too was escorting her toward the back of the house, with concern and fear in his eyes. "But it's a lovely evening," she protested.

"Safer to enjoy it from the safety of the house," Robyn retorted.

"Is it really that dangerous?" she asked Liam. "It's just wakening."

The thing in the woods screeched and wailed. "Yes," was his answer as he quickened his pace.

The cries grew louder and closer. Nora felt a chill go down her spine with the last one as they reached the stairs and both men were practically carrying her. Her knees buckled, and she nearly went face first to the deck of the porch. The air turned frigid, a dark mist came up in the woods, and Nora covered her ears. Both her companions threw themselves over her as a shield as one last screech sounded. Then the night went still.

She looked at Robyn, who was far more pale than usual. "What the hell is that thing?" she demanded.

"I don't think you really want to know, not just yet," Robyn said before standing up and locking the porch door.

Nora turned to Liam. "Care to give me a straight answer? The elf won't."

He didn't try to rise, but sat on the floor of the enclosed porch gazing at her. "That is what Winnie was supposed to train you to keep wrangled," he answered honestly. "That is a Garnel."

Jaw agape, Nora tried to speak, but her voice had vanished. Her eyes widened as she shook her head in the negative. Liam shook his in the positive. Robyn kept watch at the porch window for the creature's approach.

"I don't ever remember hearing anything like that in all the time I spent out here," she gasped out when her voice returned. She backed up until she felt the wall behind her. "Care to tell me what I'm up against?"

Liam snickered, "The house."

Robyn gave him a disdainful glance. "A Garnel is a shape shifting creature that can poison your soul just as easily as poison your body." He stared down at Nora. "They traveled here to the new land with the first ships of pilgrims. There was talk that they may have mated with the American Wendigo; however, I have my doubts. They look down on all other races, including Wendigos."

"Wendigo?" she asked in a high pitched screech.

"Lower your voice," Robyn warned sternly. "You must show no fear! It will feast on fear, and only grow stronger. When you face it you must not show fear!"

"Wake up, Robyn," she countered. "I'm not anywhere near ready to take on such a critter."

"About that she's right," an aged voice announced. "And that would be whose fault, Elf?"

Robyn winced. "Byntwig." He moved into the doorway. "What brings the troll master here?" The elf didn't look or sound pleased with the appearance of this new comrade.

"If a Garnel is at large it puts all the communities in jeopardy. Not just your precious alliance with the world of man, Robyn Goodwyn. We too have a stake in this battle," the diminutive, dark skinned man with the long white beard and amber colored eyes snarled. His long staff of gnarled wood looked very much like it could inflict harm, and he used it to force his way out to the porch. "*Saol fada chugat,*" he greeted Nora roughly.

Nora turned to Liam. "He said long life to you." Liam

said softly.

Byntwig's nose furrowed up at the interference. "I don't need a translator," he snapped.

"I do," Nora informed the troll.

Cocking his head to one side, he nearly lost his balance as the staff he carried went out from under him. "What do you mean, you need a translator?" he snarled. "My enunciation of your native tongue is perfect."

"I'm sure it is, but I don't speak Gaelic." Her tone was quiet, but not trembling. She wasn't fearful or intimidated by the troll. If anything, his presence made her feel calm.

Again the old troll nearly toppled. He turned to Robyn. "Elf, is this true?" His head and neck snapped as he whipped round to the man he'd shoved past. "She does not speak the old tongue?"

"She does not," Robyn answered resentfully. "The last Guardian never taught her. And in four weeks, she's been too lazy to learn."

"Hey," Nora barked. She quickly moved to her feet and advanced on the elf. "Don't you dare act ashamed by my lack of language skills!" she admonished. Robyn stammered, but she was done with him and turned her attentions to the troll. "I don't know who or what you are—"

"I am Byntwig, Master Troll of the Mage guild." He chuckled at her bravado. He leaned on his staff and gave her an appraising gaze.

Nora paused in her tirade, her words faded, and she blinked. "You're a troll?" He nodded. "But you don't look...."

"I'm not what you expected?" He mused. "Well, you're not my idea of a human Guardian either. I'd say we're a draw."

Her bluster abated, Nora nodded solemnly. "How do you prefer to be addressed?" she asked the troll directly, ignoring Robyn altogether. She heard Liam snort behind her and chose to ignore him as well.

Byntwig grinned. "You're under the impression that you and I are going to be conversing?"

"If I understand the situation correctly, yes," she said firmly. "I'd say you and I are going to be conversing quite a bit."

"You may call me Byntwig," he chuckled. "And you?"

"Nora." She gave him a slight curtsey, remembering her manners.

The troll's face shifted. "Woman of honor," he murmured. "Yes, fitting." He tapped his staff. "But why is it that you don't know the old tongue? How is it that the last Guardian didn't teach you?"

Casting a glance at her companions, Nora could see they were reluctant to speak. "Winnie, it seems, lost a wager with that thing out there before I was ever born." It was honest, and yet didn't give too much information, just enough to start an open dialog.

Cocking a brow upward, the troll considered her answer. "I see." He glanced at Robyn. "When you learned this truth, why is it you didn't call upon the image guild?"

"We thought we could handle it ourselves," Robyn confessed.

"You are not a mage," the old troll growled. "And neither is that shaman…neither of you own that privilege and honored title." He shook his head. "It is not for you to try and teach a mage; only a mage can train a mage, and you two well know it." Neither man seemed to be able to counter the statement nor argue with the troll, who motioned Nora closer. "So these two tried to teach you, did they?"

"Don't blame them." Nora crossed her arms, feeling defensive and protected. "They *were* trying to help."

"Loyalty," mused the troll, "Is a virtue you don't have time for, my girl. While it may serve you well in the future, we don't have time for it at the moment. For now, child, there will be only frank honesty." He shook a bony finger in her face. "You're the hope of many, not just for these two."

"What do you suggest, Master Mage?" she asked. "What they've been doing isn't working."

The troll master of magic snorted. "I can only imagine." With wise old amber eyes, he gazed into Nora's. "Been trying to force you into the elf's idea of what a Guardian is, eh?"

She nodded.

"I'll wager because of it, you don't feel the energy of the universe coursing through your veins." His old voice sounded sad and weary. "Poor child," he pitied softly as she shook her head. "Well, what do you expect? It's like asking a carpenter to sew." Tapping the staff on the floor once more, he gave her a more positive gaze and a wan smile. "We'll soon set this to rights. I know the ways of magic, and I can sense the power of magic in you."

"I take it you're here to stay," Nora sighed.

"As long as I am needed," he countered. "And not a moment longer. Your world is not mine, and my being here will not be good for the balance in the long run if I overstay my welcome."

"Balance?" She'd not heard that word used much in the last four weeks.

Again the troll snarled at the companions she'd kept. "I have four weeks to undo what they have messed up in the four weeks they've been at this." He looked at Nora. "In you I see one who is willing to learn, one who has a hidden fire burning. In you I see the potential of a great magic user. I ask only that you allow me to show you the path." He shrugged. "I cannot walk it for you, but I can show you its way."

"Sounds reasonable," she answered before warning, "But Gaelic and Latin are out. I'm an American, and I speak the broken English that is native to me."

"We don't have time for them to be properly learned," he agreed. "Later you may wish to educate yourself…that is, if you survive." He snickered wickedly.

"You're one cheerful little doomsayer, Byntwig," she observed. "All right then, come in, be welcome, and let's get started." She opened the door to her cottage, allowing the troll to enter.

Liam followed, along with Robyn. Byntwig looked about the cheerful kitchen. Nora wondered if he too was vegan, and was going to turn up his nose at feasting on animal flesh. But he didn't seem to be perturbed by the scents in the air, and proceeded to the parlor and dining rooms. Nora followed in his wake. When he entered the parlor the urn on the mantle began to shake and rock. Nora turned a questioning eye to the troll.

"She's unhappy that she's been found out, and more than a bit defensive," he explained, before advancing and pointing his staff at the urn. "Silence, you!" he shouted forcefully. "You should have given fair warning to the guild!" The urn went still. "Allowing an elf and a Celtic shaman to give training…. They are not guild members!" he admonished. "Now, be good enough to keep your opinions to yourself, woman. I have only four weeks to bring this one up to speed."

There was a groan that sounded as if it came from the urn.

"Had you the decency to contact the guild, we could have arranged for someone to coach the child!" he growled. "There are loopholes and there are loopholes."

Nora felt an urge to defend Winnie, but found she agreed with the anger coming from the old troll. She liked him instinctively, and she trusted him.

The urn went still, and Byntwig turned his back on it. "This room will serve the purpose of functioning as your classroom for the next four weeks," he addressed Nora. "I see in you a predisposition toward natural magic; your aura is strong and powerful, while your personal sense of self-worth has been…damaged. We will make this more a review of what you know deep down…and we will bolster your natural talents. Confidence will follow."

"Will it be enough?" she asked.

Byntwig sighed. "It will have to be." He motioned her to be seated. "Shall we begin?"

Nora smiled at the troll. "Sure."

Chapter 9

Nora's time was devoted to relearning and reviewing what Byntwig thought was necessary. Liam and Robyn were pressed into domestic service. The old troll dispensed with the use of Gaelic and translated most of what he could into the Anglo tongue. What couldn't be translated easily was put to the side to be learned after the dangers were over.

The old troll, it seemed, had a wealth of patience, unlike Robyn, who had been driven to distraction by Nora's lack of progress. He concentrated on the basics of magic, feeling that Nora's natural drive was the key to her survival. He was pleased that she had learned about the surrounding acres of the Hollow. Knowing the lay of the land and the plants and animals she'd be apt to encounter on a "normal" day gave her an advantage, he said. Even though her foe was familiar with the Hollow, it didn't have a working knowledge of the changes that happened during its hibernation. That advantage in her favor, and her lack of Gaelic, were strategic benefits, the troll assured her. After all, if the creature tried to sway her or lure her with Gaelic, she wasn't likely to answer.

Nora still felt like a fish out of water, just trying to do simple things. She was grateful that Byntwig didn't feel she needed to work on potions at this time. He said her mind and her ability to bend energy were more important in the battle she would be facing. Nora had her doubts that she could bend anything with more resistance than an envelope.

"I should be doing better," she complained bitterly when she was unable to make a foil propeller move. "Damn it, it won't budge."

Byntwig agreed with her, she could tell, but didn't say so. "Keep trying," he urged.

"I can't," she burst into tears. "I'm trying and trying and nothing happens." She sank to her knees, feeling drained and empty.

Liam and Robyn watched from the hall, having been banned and exiled from the parlor when Byntwig was teaching. He shot a look their way, warning without words to keep their pity and their sympathy to themselves. "Nora," Byntwig said flatly. "Try again."

Sobbing, she shook her head. "No, I'm done. I don't care! We are doomed!"

Liam moved as if he might step into the room. Byntwig motioned with his ever present staff to keep still. "I said, get up and try again," he demanded.

Nora took a long ragged breath, shakily rose to her feet, and tried once again to get the propeller to shift. It rocked, it shuddered, and then just as she thought it might finally spin, all four legs folded straight up and it fell off the pin upon which it was seated. Nora hung her head in defeat.

Byntwig rushed forward to inspect the object they'd been using. "Bless my soul," he muttered. "I've never seen anything like it."

"I failed," she whispered.

"On the contrary," Byntwig boasted. "You did what no novice has ever done. You caused it to fold." He was smiling. "That takes far more concentrated energy than merely making it spin." The old troll congratulated his apprentice. "Bravo girl, bravo."

Nora held up a hand. "I can't do more, I'm drained."

He gave her an approving nod. "You've earned a break, and an extra portion of protein. Why don't you take a walk outside in the garden to clear your mind?"

~*~

Liam watched as Nora walked silently past him toward the kitchen and the back door to the garden. "Was that unexpected?" he asked.

"Entirely," Byntwig nodded. "The girl has far more potential than we expected. She has natural abilities that are far more advanced than even the last Guardian at her prime."

"But she drains so quickly," Liam observed. He worried that the task was too great for Nora. It disturbed him that he'd been developing feelings toward her, but he was too primal to deny them. "Will she be ready, can she survive?"

"Yes, to all your questions," Byntwig stated with a cryptic smile.

~*~

Nora was thankful for the break. The cool October air and the sun in the garden were soul refreshing. In the two weeks since Byntwig had taken over her education, she'd had little opportunity to spend time in the garden. Most of the late season fruits and vegetation were harvested, leaving vines and shrubbery nearly bare. Even the apple tree had only a few hard to reach apples left on it. The summer songbirds had taken the change of the angle of the sun as a signal to head south, and only the hearty game birds and birds of prey would be left in the meadow, the swamp, and the forest.

The walk and the patio followed the natural flow of the hillside and moraine. From the garden she could see the tall grass of the meadow had lost its bright green hue, and was now headed to soft gold and brown. Cattails would be popping in the swamp soon, sending seeds everywhere. The cranes were gone, as were the egrets and the meadowlarks, and she felt a pang of regret that Winnie would miss the change of season.

She'd spent a good deal of time in the last six weeks getting acquainted with Winnie on a different level by reading her journals. She was nearly up to when Winnie had turned fifty, still years before her own birth. In the journals, she encountered facets of her aunt she'd never guessed existed. She had been aware of how much Winnie loved the cottage, but she had no idea how much she had looked forward to the change of season and the coming of fall and winter. Nor had she any idea of how many romantic escapades the other woman had experienced, here at the cottage and abroad. She envied her that. Once more her memories of Daniel flooded her mind.

Drained and emotionally exhausted, Nora edged her way down to the wall that created the defined borders of the garden. Needing to put space between herself and her companions, she moved to the lower area of the yard. Her head was throbbing, as it often did when she was physically drained. She was glad that Byntwig was as commanding a force as he was. Between him and Liam, Robyn had given up trying to purge her. But the elf was still giving her grief over not speaking any of the "accepted" magical tongues, and she had a feeling he was putting fillers in the meat portions that Byntwig and Liam had demanded. If she could prove it….

She sat down on the wall that separated the house and garden from the nature preserve that comprised the rest of the property. Pulling her feet up to rest on the wide flat top, she placed her chin on her upraised knees. She wondered why Byntwig was excited about the foil folding. The goal had been getting the damn thing to spin. She was miserable, and felt like a failure.

Pouting and moping on the wall, she began to feel like she wasn't quite as alone as she'd planned to be. She looked toward the house and garden. She didn't see any of her companions coming to keep her company or fuss at her. Her eyes moved toward the stand of trees just beyond the garden wall. Nora became aware that there was something there, something watching her intently. She let her eyes scan upward through the tree's large branches, and spotted a figure lounging in the crotch of two branches. The hair on the back of her neck began to tingle. What she saw didn't belong there.

Nora didn't need to ask; she knew who and what he was, but she asked anyway. "Who are you and want do you want?"

He could have stepped out of any of the fantasy or romance novels she'd read over the years. His rugged face was chiseled, and could have graced a movie screen. He was clean shaven, and his dark hair was worn long and tied back. Dark eyes, black as night, were observing her with mild interest. She could see that he was powerfully built, and comfortable in his own skin. He was dressed in dark garments. Nora had the impression that the garments were an illusion; that they would vanish if the creature wished it so.

Nora didn't think he was going to answer her…he didn't seem inclined. Then he opened his mouth. "I've been called by many names." His voice was deep, rich, and full of resonance and quality. Not what she'd expected after hearing the wails, howls, and shrieks for the last two weeks. However, instinct told her this was her foe in its human guise. "Too many to recall."

"Really," she said, trying not to sound too interested. "How nice."

He inclined his head to one side. "What would you like to call me?" he inquired solicitously.

"What makes you think I have an interest in calling you anything?"

"For the sake of polite conversation," he mused.

Nora considered the suggestion, rejected it, and said blandly, "You're the Garnel."

"That is true," he admitted with a tone that was full of male pride. "However, that is not a name. As I understand it, you mortals are very fond of names and naming objects." He swung one leg down. "I'm only too happy to provide you the opportunity to fulfill your heart's desire."

Tired, cranky, and unwilling to play, Nora glared at the man form of the Garnel in the tree. "I hope you've got better lines than that, because it's not workin'."

A cheeky smile came to the handsome face. "I have a great many lines," he assured her. "Some work better than others."

"How nice for you." Nora placed her chin back on her knees and hands and closed her eyes, ignoring him. The wall was pleasant, and it wouldn't be long before it would be too cold to enjoy. The fact that she was thinking of autumn turning to winter amused her. If she failed there'd be no seasons, no world.

"What are you doing?" he asked inquisitively.

"Resting," she answered.

"Resting," he repeated. "I sit here above you…your sworn foe…and you're resting?" Nora heard the hint of irritation, and knew he was feeling insulted.

"Shhhh," she warned.

"Never has one shushed me," he said slowly.

Nora looked up; the male form was once more lounging and watching her with curiosity. "Can't you just go back to where ever it is you go during the day?"

"I have no wish to," he answered, with no trace of emotion or interest or guile.

"I am not going to tag you with some mortal name… you're a Garnel, plain and simple," she warned him crossly. "So Garnel, why don't you just let me be?"

He smiled. "That would defeat the purpose of my presence." His leg draped down over the tree, swinging lazily.

~*~

Robyn had brewed some soothing tea and had taken the pot and a mug out to the garden for Nora. He looked about the usual places that she took solace and found that she was nowhere to be found. He placed the tray with the teapot and mug on the table and began to look around the garden walk, panicking as he did so. From the ridge he could see her seated on the wall and conversing. His elf eyes searched the area and saw to whom she was talking, and the panic in his being rose. "Nora," he gasped. A staff was thrust before him, preventing him from racing to her rescue. He turned to glare at the owner of the staff. "Byntwig, I must save her...."

"No," the troll said forcefully. "If she is going to fail, we best know it now, and bring another here to keep the beastie trapped."

"You would sacrifice the girl?"

Byntwig's amber eyes flashed. "Fond as I am of this mortal, and I am fond of her, I would sacrifice my own *daughter* to keep that beast trapped."

~*~

"You don't look like the last Guardian," he remarked. "She was...interesting."

"So sorry to disappoint you." His condescending tone was grating, but less so than she'd put up with from Connie over the years. His insult had not even dented her. And sitting there on the wall, she didn't feel nearly as tired as she had.

"She had a quality," he observed. "She took great pleasure in her own being."

"Blah blah blah," Nora grumbled, with her head firmly planted on her knees. The air was filling with soft scents — grass, earth, water — and she was taking them all in.

"You're going to be no match for me," he mused. "Why bother? My argument is not, after all, with you. Why prolong the misery you seem to be in?"

"Go soak your head," she whispered softly, refreshed by

the energies of the Hollow itself. A moment later there was silence. She looked up and the tree was empty.

~*~

Robyn gasped. "Did you see that?" He turned to the troll, who was smiling from ear to ugly ear. "The Garnel moved away...." He was following the creature's movement. "He's headed...toward the wetlands?" What happened next drew from the elf a sound he seldom made. "By the seven pillars... he's dunking his head in the water...."

The troll snorted. "I wonder what it was our little Guardian in training said." Grabbing hold of the elf, he directed him back to the house. "I'd say it's safe to let her be. Come now... brew me some of that fine tea."

~*~

Nora heard a strange howl; a hint of a smile of satisfaction crossed her lips. Perhaps, just perhaps, all the hard work that the troll had made her do would pay off after all. The garden wall beneath her vibrated, and she allowed the energy to surge within her.

Chapter 10

Liam was waiting for her when she came strolling up the winding garden path, "You look like a cat who's had a canary," he announced.

"I feel like it too." She pulled the rubber band that held her hair to the nape of her neck. "It's rather a good feeling."

"Have you been picking on something bigger than yourself?" he asked with a wicked grin.

"Could be," she teased.

When she passed him, he gave her rump a playful thump, and she laughed.

Byntwig was seated in the garden. She moved to where he sat and knelt beside him. The old troll placed a hand to her face. "Do you know what you did?"

"No," she said honestly. "I know what I said, but I don't know how I made it happen."

"And how does that feel?"

"Like, at long last, I'm making real progress," she admitted in a much more positive frame of mind.

"Don't get cocky," he warned, fearing she was about to overstep.

"Cocky," she giggled. "Don't you worry, old troll, I'm still scared stiff!" She stood up, the wind playing with her hair. "I was damned lucky just now; don't think I don't know it. I know I made it happen, I just don't know how."

"We must work harder," Byntwig said carefully. "We must learn what it is that triggers the natural talent you have." He pulled at the beard on his chin. "What was it you felt just before you sent him back to his swamp?"

"He pissed me off," she said.

"Raw emotions," he said. The old troll advised, "Stay pissed off."

~*~

Nora heard the creature howling that night. For some reason he was keeping his distance. She knew there had been nights when he'd prowled near her garden wall, as if it kept him out somehow. Tonight he was out in the woods, and the sound seemed to echo in the moraine. Sitting up in the bed and listening, she thought he sounded angrier than usual.

He, she thought. She wondered if the creature had a gender or if it just chose whichever it needed when it needed. Something the old troll had said echoed something Winnie had written. Both had her puzzled. She got up, pulled her robe on, and moved down the stairs. She knew exactly which of the journals contained the passage, and she wanted to read it again. Her fingers leafed through pages swiftly, and when she found the words she read them over and over. Nora moved to the overstuffed chair…the words were not quite as she'd remembered, but close enough.

~*~

The howls ceased just before dawn, when Robyn came down to begin breakfast. He sensed her before he saw her asleep in the chair. Her face seemed more peaceful than he'd seen it in weeks. She had changed, but not all of the changes were for the better, he feared. However, they were changes that had to be made. He left her to slumber on, and wondered when it was she'd risen and what it was that she had been reading.

~*~

The aroma of coffee, good hot black coffee, caught her by surprise. Robyn didn't like to make coffee, referring to it as a devil's brew. But just the same, this morning there was coffee in the air. She opened her eyes and stretched. The sun was just beginning to filter into the windows…it was going to be another of those rare fall days. Storms would be coming soon enough, but for now she could enjoy the crisp air and clear skies.

Liam descended the stairs and met up with her in the hall on his way toward the magical aroma of coffee. "Good morning," he greeted her.

"Morning," she replied. "Someone made coffee," she observed.

"There's hope for him yet," Liam chuckled.

Expecting to find Robyn hard at work over breakfast, the pair was astounded when they saw the elf tied to a chair. The troll was seated across from him with a plate of crispy bacon before him. "Good morning," he greeted them.

Nora looked at the pitiful elf. "Was that necessary?"

Ignoring the question, the troll raised the plate of bacon. "Lovely bacon and eggs," he offered.

Liam took no notice of Robyn; he sat down and began to help himself to the meat laden meal. "What, no sausages this morning?"

Byntwig chuckled. "They are in the broiler."

"You two are just going to stuff your faces," Nora chided.

"Would you prefer twigs and berries?" Byntwig inquired with a raised brow.

Guiltily, Nora took a seat beside Liam. "No," she admitted. "I prefer bacon and eggs, thank you."

Byntwig filled a plate for her with eggs, cheese, bacon, and thick slices of buttered toast. "I caught this one," he poked a fork toward Robyn, "cutting our protein portions." He stood up, moved to the stove, and with care took out the golden brown sausages. "No wonder you're behind, he's been starving you."

Shoveling the bright fluffy eggs into her mouth, Nora shook her head. "Purging, he calls it," she corrected.

"I warned him," Byntwig went on, "That he was dealing with forces he does not understand…blasted vegan." Liam savored the food that hadn't been tampered with. Byntwig glared at the elf. "He's been giving you meat substitutes and fillers for weeks."

Nora continued to enjoy her breakfast. "He doesn't know any better."

Liam shrugged, but kept his opinion to himself.

When the meal had been consumed and everyone was satisfied, Byntwig released the elf. "From now on you will not skimp on protein!" warned the old troll.

"Winnie appreciated a good purging," he answered defensively, and made himself something to eat.

"Winnie was fully trained by the time you came into her life," the old troll shouted.

~*~

Nora looked up from the journal she'd been reading since after breakfast. The sounds of a car's brakes drew her attention, "We've got company," she warned her companions. Rising from the chair, she wondered who could be calling on her. Moments later the bell rang, and she casually moved to the door to answer it. "Yes?" She didn't unlatch the screen, but stood with the wooden door to the house rather like a shield.

Standing on the porch, clipboard in hand, was an official from the county. He had an official looking badge and photo ID. "County Inspector," he announced gruffly. "We got a report of a woman living in unhealthy conditions."

"I'll just bet you did." Nora could think of only one person who would want to cause her this kind of trouble. Still, she didn't move to unlatch the door.

The man seemed perturbed she wasn't responding, allowing him access. "I have to inspect the premises to see if this house is habitable." Still she made no move. "It's the law, lady. And if you interfere I can have this place condemned without inspecting it."

"I see." She shook her head in disgust. "So you get to interrupt my daily routine, and I have no choice but to allow it." Exhaling in frustration, Nora reached forward, unlatched the screen door, and bid him enter as she opened the door. "What would you like to see?"

He looked about the straight as a pin foyer. "Do you have

a basement?" he asked. When she nodded, he made a note on his board. "I'd like to start there, as that's where most of the household mechanicals usually are."

"Fine." She led the way to the door in the back hall that opened to the stairs down to the basement of the cottage. Most of the walls were rough stone and mortar; the floor was a plain poured floor over what had been dirt. "My great aunt didn't use this space," she said as she switched on the lights. "She didn't even like to store things in here." The man didn't seem to be listening, he moved to the furnace. He had a red inked note on his ledger that Nora saw as he passed her. "The furnace was replaced two years ago; so was the water heater and the air conditioner system. All are serviced on a regular basis, and have tags with the latest stamps of inspection."

The man frowned and read the tag on the furnace stating it had been given a maintenance check during the past summer. He made a note. He looked at the water heater and made another note. Then he looked at the venting. "No washer or dryer down here?" he asked gruffly.

"No, the washer and dryer are upstairs on a service porch," Nora answered.

"I see." He made another notation. "I'll have to inspect that too...." He looked about. "Where's your electrical panel?"

Nora pointed back toward the stairs and the metal cabinet that was on the wall.

"Fuses?" he asked.

"Breakers," Nora corrected politely. "My great aunt Winnie had the entire electrical system redone about fifteen years ago. She was very keen on keeping the house up to code."

"I'll be the judge of that," he said rather roughly.

"Of course you will."

She watched as he opened the box, looked over the complex setup, and frowned. Nora had a feeling he was on a witch hunt, but she wasn't about to tip her hand just yet.

"You say your washer and dryer are on a service porch?" He looked at her. "Out in the open?"

"Not exactly. My aunt liked being able to look out at the woods when she was doing laundry. It was easier to carry clothes out to the lines in the summer from the enclosed service porch." Nora kept her tone mild and polite, but she felt the air about her fill with an electrical surge.

"I'll be looking at that setup now," he said gruffly.

"Certainly," she nodded, and preceded him up to the main floor again. "This way," she said, showing him through the kitchen to the back porch.

Robyn was standing at the sink peeling tomatoes when they passed through.

"How many people live in this house?" the man asked.

"Just me," Nora answered. "For now."

"And the person at the sink?"

"An out of town guest." She kept the answer short. "Visiting me."

"A guest?"

"Yes," she nodded as she opened the door to the back enclosed porch. "The washer is at this end of the porch." She motioned toward the laundry. "Aunt Winnie had cabinets put up for her convenience." She motioned to the cabinets above a rather plain washer and dryer that sat beside a single tub utility sink. "She had the porch reinforced so that it would bear the weight of a fully loaded washer or a sinkful of water and whatever."

"This is not the usual setup," he said, sounding as if he'd found a chink in the armor of the house, something he could use.

"No, it's not." Nora opened the cabinet. "But she did get a variance to have it set up this way." Her hand reached in and took out a clear plastic sleeve that contained a rather legal looking document. "She had the porch inspected every two years to make sure it stayed in good condition. No termites, no other bugs either."

The man frowned.

"Would you care to inspect the root cellar?" Nora asked gently.

He turned to glare at her. "Do you think this is a joke?"

"No," she said firmly. "I think that someone has decided that since I won't sell my house to them, they are going to try and trump up some phony complaint and force me out." His eyes opened wide, and she added, "But I think the county president might not be very happy with whoever is wasting valuable county resources. I intend to report the person responsible to the realtor's association." She crossed her arms. "As well as anyone who is in cahoots with her."

The man shook his head. "Lady, this was not my idea."

"I didn't think it was," she acknowledged. "You're as much a victim in this as I am. In short, you're a scapegoat to cover someone else's tracks."

He wrote something up, signed it, and handed it to her. "No violations," he told her contritely.

"Thank you." She accepted the paper, escorting him

through the house once more and out the front door. She stayed on the porch and watched him leave. Liam joined her on the porch when the car was on its way down the drive.

"What was that all about?" he inquired.

"Connie," Nora answered in exasperation.

"Connie?"

Nora explained, "She wants me to sell this place, and is refusing my refusal. So she's trying to force my hand."

"Why?"

Pointing to the woods, the young woman said, "The woods surrounding us belong to the county. There are a few places that don't...they were settled before the county took over the woods...and wetlands. Up the road is what's left of a toboggan sled hill. But more and more folks are using this area in winter for cross country skiing and other winter entertainment. There's this big time developer who wants to build a four seasons resort, and my hundred acres would make a very nice part of that plan."

"You were aware of these developers' intentions?"

"Anyone who reads would be," she snorted. "However, I doubt my cousin would credit me with that much intelligence."

A firm hand caressed her cheek. "None so blind?" he asked.

"Something like that," she agreed. His hand on her skin gave her a feeling of bonding. More and more she was finding herself drawn to this mysterious stranger sent to "test" her mettle.

Liam reluctantly withdrew his hand. "Byntwig went out the back way while you had that official in the house. The fewer who know we're here...."

"The better," she agreed. Feeling his withdrawal, she turned her face toward the direction the car had gone down the driveway. "At least the Garnel didn't bother with that county inspector...that's all I'd need."

The dark eyed gypsy studied her. "Do you think your cousin is going to give us more trouble?"

"Oh yes, you can count on it," she nodded. "Connie's not the kind to let it rest until she's got what she wants." Nora made sure not to make eye contact with the man, unable to shake the urges he was generating. "I think I'd better give our friend Mr. Benton, Winnie's lawyer, a call this morning. It's time to cut Connie off at the pass." She moved past the shaman, keeping herself very tight.

~*~

Miles Benton seemed surprised to hear from her. "I had thought you'd be busy getting settled in."

Nora sat in her favorite chair, the phone cradled in her lap. "I should be, but I had a rather unhappy visit this morning from someone in the county inspections office."

"What on earth for?"

"*Someone* trying to get my house condemned."

"I beg your pardon." He sounded taken aback. "Winnie was always very good about keeping the house up to code. In fact, as far as I know she went above and beyond."

"I think Connie put a bug in someone's ear. You know she's got friends all over in high places, thanks to our grandfather's contacts," Nora suggested. "This guy didn't seem happy about not finding any violations, or the fact that I was onto the scheme."

"You really think Connie would go that far?" he asked.

"I suppose that's why Winnie insisted on the maintenance upgrades."

"Connie must think I'm oblivious to who her clients are," Nora suggested. "I've known about the developers out here for the last two years or better. Winnie refused to even speak with them."

"She did more than refuse," joked the lawyer. "She had two surveyors tossed in jail for outright trespassing."

"Is there any way we can put a stop to or impede Connie's efforts?" she asked.

"There may be a few. Give me a day to make some calls on your behalf, Miss Belfry," he said, sounding very official.

"That's what I pay you for," she said, sounding more like Winnie than herself.

"Yes, it is."

Nora sat in the chair after she'd hung up, the phone still cradled in her lap. Byntwig returned to the house and studied her. "Tell me about this cousin," he inquired quietly. He moved to sit in the chair across from her.

"What's to tell?" Nora asked, and sighed deeply. "Connie is older, smarter, and richer...or was *richer* until Aunt Winnie left everything to me. I don't think she has any idea of the extent of Winnie's wealth. After all, Winnie didn't live the way Connie would expect a person of means to live. She looked at Aunt Winnie the way one does an eccentric relation they'd rather not admit was part of their family."

The old troll pulled at his snowy beard. "How would this Connie expect a person of means to live?"

Closing her eyes, Nora sighed and said, "Connie's idea of living is rooted in the city. She's got clients who live in penthouses atop tall buildings, with a million dollar view of the city and the lakefront."

The troll wore a cunning smile; he could understand the desire to live above the minions of the city, his own home being in a tower. "It's not a bad way to spend one's time."

Nora kept her eyes closed; her mind's eye had conjured up the image of Winnie taking her for a walk in the woods. "No, but it wasn't Winnie's way," she contended. "Winnie was a child of nature, happier when she was in the woods than when she had to be in the city. The buildings suffocated her, she used to say." She remembered her aunt lovingly. "Winnie knew more about the moraines than some of the so called experts. She could track how many bird species were on the property at any given time, she knew what herds of deer and elk were here and if their numbers had grown or declined…and if the winter was going to be rough or mild."

"Do you have those skills?"

"Not like she did," Nora conceded. "But, I did learn a great deal from her during those summers I spent here." Her face flushed with color. "I hate to admit it, but I really enjoyed it when it was just me and Winnie. When Connie and David weren't here. It was easier to learn from Winnie when they weren't here being a distraction."

"Why would that be?"

Nora looked over at the old troll. "Because Connie always made me feel inferior to her." The face of the troll gave little away; his weathered features were always a bit of a mask. "Connie's folks always had lots of money. My dad didn't. He was the youngest son, and had a thing about not asking the family for help if he didn't have to. He worked for the family business until he became too ill. Daddy hid his illness for a very long time, and when he couldn't any longer he and Mother sold everything they had here property wise, kept the stocks and bonds, and moved. I was in college. A local, small named college. Connie went to a big named school, and never lets anyone forget it. She never lets anyone forget that she's got a masters and I don't. Connie always had the best of everything; the best clothes, the best car, the best boyfriend…." A pained note sounded.

"Boyfriend?"

"Mine," Nora admitted with sorrow. "Or so I thought at the time."

The troll nodded in sympathy. "Go on."

"During the summers that Connie and David weren't present, I was free to be more myself." She closed her eyes again. "Winnie never made me feel like a plain Jane. She never cared if I was wearing designer jeans and big named shoes. She concentrated on educating my mind and my soul." Her face became peaceful. "There's not a plant or flower or creature that is in our Hollow that I don't know. I know every inch of the Hollow!"

"Say that again," the troll demanded.

"Say what?" Nora opened her eyes. "That I know every inch of the Hollow?"

"Bless my soul," the old troll crowed. "The Guardian found a loophole."

Chapter 11

Nora had her doubts when the old mentor asked her to take him on a guided tour of the Hollow, starting with her garden. After an hour of touring and reaching only the garden wall, he called a halt. He marched back up to the house, calling for the elf and Liam. Nora shook her head and took a seat on the wall. Something, some inner sense, told her she wasn't alone. "What do you want, Garnel?"

"My freedom," the Garnel answered coldly.

Looking over her shoulder, she watched as he kept a respectful distance. "And what would you do with that freedom?"

"Make those who placed me in this prison suffer," he said with a smile.

~*~

"That does not strike me as a recommendation for allowing you to go free," she said flatly.

The Garnel gave her a wicked grin. "No, I don't suppose

it does." He leaned on a tree, still keeping his distance, but was close enough to converse. "This is not your battle...why take it up?"

"Who says it's not my battle?" He paused; he hadn't thought the mousy creature would participate in a battle of wits. Nora shook her head and gave him an annoyed gaze. "You don't even know me."

"No," he said equally crossly. "I never had the pleasure, as I've been relegated to hibernation during your visits." He stayed close to the tree, but mentally put out feelers to sense what it was that made the girl tick. He drew back sharply when he came up against the boundary of the wall.

"Daylight," she said softly. "You can't cross the wall during the day." Her eyes sparkled with mischief. "Not even mentally."

"Bitch," he muttered.

"Sometimes," she agreed.

Composing himself and his thoughts, he gave her a wan smile. "But that is not your doing, now is it?"

"I suppose you think you're charming," she observed. "But it's wasted on me." She stood up. "My heart is in an iron maiden."

The Garnel watched with wide eyes as she strolled away unhurriedly.

~*~

Byntwig gave the girl time. He had known the Garnel was present, and wanted to see what her reaction to him would be, as well as his to her. "She's a strange little creature," he observed to Liam, standing at his side. "Unaware of her own natural presences. For years she's only seen herself as a plain

Jane."

"That may work to her advantage," Liam agreed.

"It must be very frustrating for the Garnel," chuckled the old troll. "He's used to human females falling all over themselves when he pays them the least amount of attention."

"Nora only finds him aggravating," Liam mused.

"Still, she is just a woman," warned the troll. "Fond of her as I may be, and I am fond of her, she is only a woman. If she fails, both sides of the mists will be in danger."

"Are you fond of her?" Liam asked. "I know I am, and I shouldn't be. My only task was to test her mettle." He shook his head. "I should have returned to the Fillip. I should be preparing them for the chance of her failing. Yet here I remain, working to prepare her for a battle that seems impossible for her to win."

"Both you and the elf are fond of her in your own manner and way. Not that the elf would admit it," the troll stated.

"My feelings for her are unimportant." He shrugged. "I am here as a mentor; once she is truly a Guardian I will return to my realm and that will be that. You and the elf are free to come and go. My coming was only because I am a mage, and you two are not."

"But you wouldn't raise a hand to save her, would you?"

"No," Byntwig admitted. "She must stand or fall...I cannot control her destiny."

Liam stood up and walked to the edge of the patio. "I would."

The old troll warned. "You shouldn't."

~*~

Nora looked up to see Liam watching her, and her heart

beat a little faster. *Stop being silly,* she warned herself. *He's just here to make sure you can beat old Garnel.*

"Did you have a nice walk?" he asked.

"Ran into Garnel," she said edgily. "He really thinks he's something." She shook her head. "He acts as if he expects me to jump over the wall and throw myself into his arms."

"And you don't wish to?"

She made a sour face. "God, no." She shuddered. "He's a bit smarmy for my tastes." Liam seemed shocked for an instant, and then tossed back his head and roared with laughter. Nora moved past him. "I mean really, all that goo and longing looks. Who does he think he's fooling?"

~*~

Liam turned to Byntwig. "She's something the Garnel has never come up against; a woman impervious to his charms."

The old troll grinned. "There are many levels to our little novice…pity time is so short. I should like to know more of her fiber." He sniffed the air. "That elf is at it again…I don't smell any meat."

A moment later the elf came rushing out the door, just being missed by the broom chasing him out on its own. "And stay out of my kitchen," Nora shouted.

Guiltily, Robyn looked at Liam. "I was just making a nice lunch."

"Vegan," Liam said coyly.

"Well… yes…." Robyn admitted.

The three men took seats on the patio, not wishing to incur more of Nora's wrath. Byntwig glanced about the garden space. "Miss Winnie and her predecessors had a good eye for keeping within the bounds of nature." He pointed to the natural flow of the land on the moraine. "See how they followed the land instead of trying to make it bend to their will?"

"You're making a point?" Liam asked.

Robyn crossed his arms, "So, they did one thing right."

Tapping his staff on the ground, the old troll spoke sharply. "The Belfry Guardians are not like any other; not even like other *human* guardians." His amber eyes moved to the house. "Not in how they choose to live, not in how they use the gift of the power that surges within them. We must keep that in mind as we prepare Nora for her battle."

Robyn stood up and paced like a caged cat. "She's nowhere near ready for any kind of battle," he said bitterly. "She can't do the simplest of incantations. Her lack of understanding of Gaelic and Latin hampers her from reading the oldest of scrolls! She doesn't seem able to focus. She's lazy and undisciplined." He didn't hide his disappointment or his disdain. "I blame Winnie for all of this!"

Liam was more reflective. "While it's true the girl is behind," his voice softened, becoming almost sentimental. "She does have heart, and she's trying."

"My concern," Byntwig announced, "is her lack of confidence."

Robyn sneered. "What does she have to be confident over? She's a hot mess!"

The old troll shook his head. "How can you mentor her with so much resentment? Winnie isn't the only one at fault for the girl's lack of progress!"

Robyn's mouth dropped open.

Liam cleared his throat, distracting the two from beginning

a battle of words that would leave no winner. "From what I saw of the interactions between her and this cousin Connie, I can understand why she's lacking confidence. That woman is heartless in her dealings with Nora. She rudely came into the house without an invitation, practically demanding that Nora sign it over to her. One can only imagine what the rest of the family's treatment of Nora has been over the years." He seemed to be thinking of something that happened during the exchange, but kept it to himself.

"Nora has told me that the men of the family had no respect for her father, and allowed their feelings to trickle down to her, whether it was right or not." Byntwig leaned on his staff. "We must work on helping her build the confidence a Guardian needs."

~*~

The rest of the day Nora kept busy in the study, reading more of the journals. Little by little she felt she was beginning to understand her aunt. Winnie was more complex than her lawyer had guessed. Winnie had adventures the family seemed to know nothing about, and a list of suitors all over the world. The gifts they'd given the old girl took on new meaning to Nora. If Winnie could have men from the four corners of the world chasing her, it gave Nora hope of someday being just as desirable, if only to one man. She wished the one that her heart was longing for was free. But as he wasn't, she'd just have to hope that one just as good would one day show up. Just because she hadn't had much luck with love up to now didn't mean her entire future was cast in stone. Perhaps there would be one man just for her.

~*~

Nora awoke early the next morning with a feeling she couldn't shake; she wondered what Connie was going to try now that her county inspector had failed to find violations. If there was one thing Nora was sure of, it was that Connie wasn't about to give up what she considered her due. This property wasn't anything to Connie but a dollar sign. Taking it away from Nora made it all the sweeter, Nora was sure. Trouble was coming. Connie wasn't about to allow a little thing like the county inspector's failure to stop her. Nora was going to have to prepare not only to do battle with the thing in the Hollow, but with Connie. And part of her dreaded Connie more than that thing.

The air coming in the open window of the bedroom was crisp, fresh, and full of fragrances. The sun was not yet up, and the room was still dim. She sat up in the bed that had once been Winnie's. Everything in the house, most everything, had been Winnie's, or Harriet's before her, but everything here was family heirlooms. Nora envied them; the Belfry women had been women with self-determination and independence, while still maintaining good relationships with the family.

Nora began to ruminate over the family history, as she knew it. Winnie's brother, her grandfather John, had never been all that fond of Nora. He more or less tolerated her, the child of his youngest son. For that matter, the old man had never seemed all that fond of Nora's dad or her mother. It was as if he'd held her father's illness against him, a sign of weakness. Uncle John was his natural favorite, followed by Aunt Mary Kate. Her cousin John *the third* was of course the top notch of the grandchildren, and had been a teen when Nora was born. She was still troubled that neither father nor son had seen fit to be at the reading of Winnie's will. However, since neither had voiced an objection to her inheritance, she thought it was best to let that sleeping dog be. She had a feeling that neither had the slightest idea of what Winnie owned outside of the stock to the family business.

Granddad John Belfry had been a powerful businessman, and his son was following in his footsteps, as was his son. The Belfry foundry was one of the oldest and best established in the Chicago area, and it was a name to be trusted, a brand that had withstood the march of time. The company was sound and strong in this new century because of leadership like Uncle John's, and now cousin John's. Granddad John's will had been generous, but it had shown favoritism to some others in the family more than to Nora or her parents. It was no secret that the old man had preferred John the third to all, and then Connie and David over Nora. Grandmother Agatha had admonished him at several family functions, only to be told the world wouldn't be fair, why should he be? He had a good point, Nora's father had said...the world wouldn't be fair. Life wasn't fair, but that's the way it was.

Winnie was not in favor nor had she ever been, and it never seemed to bother her, not even when her brother had died and left her nothing. Nora had never really cared before about any of this, and wondered why she was so wrapped up in it now. She wondered if it was because of her strong links to Winnie, or that her parents were so far away. Family, her little unit of family, meant the world to her.

Edward Belfry, her father, was a quiet man compared to Uncle John. He didn't look much like his father or his brother. Edward was slight of build, and had an elegance that no one else in the family could claim...he moved as if he were constantly in a magical dance. He even looked more Edwardian than the other men in the family, and Winnie had made comments on it more than once. Nora's father was well read and traveled, having served in the navy before settling down with his childhood sweetheart. Nora's parents were a rare love story, and even after nearly thirty years of marriage were still devoted to one another. Theirs was the kind of love that Nora wanted for herself, but she knew that her engagement to Daniel had fallen far short...it was an embarrassment. And that, too, went back to Connie.

A chill ran through her when she thought of the man she'd been set to marry. She'd not thought about him in quite a while until she'd inherited the cottage. Now, in the manner of six weeks, thoughts of Daniel McGowan had come into her mind several times. She counted her blessings for having found out what a bounder he was before she'd taken vows that would have chained her to him. Winnie had called him a serpent the first time she'd been introduced to him, and had tried to warn Nora off. To her shame she hadn't taken her great aunt seriously. Her parents had also been uncomfortable with the union, and had begged her to rethink accepting his proposal. Uncle John, on the other hand, had been uncharacteristically supportive. For the first time in many years, Nora began to wonder why. There had been no reason for Uncle John to be so supportive, was there?

Daniel McGowan was not the kind of man Nora had dated before. He was unlike anyone in her life. Looking back, Nora could see that they made a very odd pairing indeed. Her mousy quietness and his larger than life way of attacking life just didn't seem to be very well blended; he eclipsed her. He was the kind of man most girls dreamed of...tall, dark, and handsome, and well connected. He was older than Nora, and worked in the same real-estate offices that Connie had started in. In fact, it had been Connie who introduced them. She could still remember the sound of his rich baritone and perfect diction. See his sculpted facial features, with those big brown eyes and all that wavy dark hair...his strong arms, his muscular build...and that wonderful heady scent that always seemed to linger when he was there. Yet looking back, she was now aware of things she'd allowed to go unnoticed.

She had fallen head over heels for him, there was no denying it. He had played her like a harp, knowing all the notes that would entice her. He could speak about art without sounding jaded or put on. He knew music, and could follow a score; he knew literature and had read many of the same books that she had...or so she'd been led to believe. Had she really been so desperate for love that she'd not taken into consideration that he wasn't all she'd thought he was? Had she not seen the unmistakable signs of him not being truthful? She should have seen that he'd been coached in the things that she was interested in. Finding out it was all a ruse had broken her heart and her spirit. Knowing it had all been a setup by Connie had only topped the betrayals. She had never been sure why she hadn't told the entire family the truth, but she'd kept Connie's secret.

Slipping out of the bed, she gazed at her reflection in the looking glass and found herself lacking. She wasn't shapely or exotic looking like Connie. She was mousy in comparison, and had been a late bloomer. In fact, Nora wasn't sure she'd bloomed yet. Her hair was baby fine, and lacked the luster in color compared to Connie's thick, lush, dark chocolate hair. She didn't dress with the same flare or style; she didn't have the skills at doing makeup that Connie abundantly possessed. She was deficient...she lacked Connie's wall of confidence that said she could take on the world and leave it in her wake. Nora was small and insignificant, hardly the warrior the world needed at this time.

"Winnie, what did you see in me?" she asked aloud. "Why put this on my shoulders?"

With less than fourteen days left, Nora wasn't sure she could save the world. Worse, she wasn't even sure she wanted to. It was a heavy burden, one that couldn't be shared. Not with her parents, not with anyone in the family. While she was grateful for the support of her mentors, she couldn't share this burden with them. They were not the Guardian of the Hollow...she was. Or at least she was supposed to be. She wished she felt more like a Guardian, instead of a failure.

"Some Guardian you are," she scoffed, looking at her reflection. "You're a phony, a fake, a...a bogus counterfeit imitation of what a Guardian is supposed to be." The old childhood insecurities that she'd buried years before rose to the surface, and she felt the same rush of apprehension and terror she'd felt as a child. She experienced an urge to run to her favorite hiding place, the attic of the cottage. Whenever Connie or David's taunts had become too much, she would come up here to Winnie's room, creep into the closet, and use the hidden door that led to the attic room just above the master bedroom. Connie and David didn't know about the hatch...Winnie never told them. It was their shared secret, just Winnie's and Nora's. A private place for Nora to go when things got to be too much, and she needed that right now.

Pushing her clothes that now hung in the closet aside, she reached back until her fingers touched the latch. If you didn't know how to use it, it would never open. Nora knew more about the cottage than anyone else, with perhaps the exception of Winnie. She knew all the secret panels that the original Belfry inhabitant had installed. Some weren't even in the blueprints; others were not what they seemed to be. Over the years, only the person inhabiting the house was left to know about them. Such as the secret of the bookcase that swung out to reveal a safe. Or the hidden room behind the pantry. This staircase, the only way up to the little room in the attic, was one of the house's best kept secrets. Even in the dark Nora knew her way, and didn't have to depend on flashlights or candles.

At the top of the stairs was a little landing, and a door framed in oak with carved oak leaves and acorns. Nora rested her head on the door for a moment before turning the crystal knobbed handle. It wasn't locked…there was no key to this space; it was so secret there had never been a reason to have a lock on the door.

Just inside the door was a switch. When it was turned on a pretty miniature crystal chandelier lit the space with soft, warm glowing light, casting little rainbows on the walls from the crystal prisms. The soft sage green walls were decorated with terracotta symbols; the black and white tiled floor also was in a pattern that Nora had never taken much notice of before. But it was all familiar, and it felt safe, comforting, and secure, like a hug from Aunt Winnie. This was where Winnie had told her the most precious secret possessions of her life were kept.

The trunk that held her beautiful gowns from her centennial tour was here, draped with a lace shawl. A little bistro table in cast iron, but painted to look like weathered bronze and its matching chairs, was still in the corner, set for tea, just as it had been when Nora was a child. A wooden bookshelf with photo albums that held tin-types and yellowed photos of relations that were nearly forgotten beckoned her to come and remember her heritage. A few things had been added over the years…more trunks, a second bookshelf, more symbols on the walls…but it was still her safe place. Under the glow of the chandelier she took a seat at the table. When she had, she noticed an envelope with her name on it in Winnie's hand sitting on the table. She hadn't expected to find anything like it up here. She opened the letter and read the words.

Dearest Nora,

Forgive me for not having prepared you for the task that awaits you. By now you've been contacted by an elf and a shaman…and with any luck a mage. God and Goddess help us if it is one of the trolls…they are not always the most benevolent or supportive of their human counterparts. However, if it is a troll I pray it be one of the most talented ones, for you are going to need someone who thinks outside the box.

I cannot tell you how to go about the task that lies ahead. In my foolish youth I lost the right to give you the weapons and training that are your due, and your birthright. But I will tell you this, Nora; you are up to this task. Never, never doubt yourself, my sweet child.

You are a Belfry, and much stronger than you know. There are deep roots to the magic that races in your being. I've seen it, and I have always known that you were the one to follow me.

If you have come to this room, it is because you know it will give you what it always has; courage and strength and knowledge. It was always my safe haven, and I'm so glad it was yours as well.

Think kindly of me when I cross your mind; take from this room what you need. Be the Guardian of Misty Hollow, as you were always meant to be. Let nothing stand in your way! Let nobody stop you...you are up to this.

With love,
Aunt Winnie

"Take from this room what I need?" she asked herself aloud. "What's here?" She looked about. "What game are you playing with me now, Winnie?" Winnie had loved to play hidden item games when Nora was a child. She wondered if this was one of them, or still part of the last game they had played together. "What's up here?" she repeated, but this time she was looking about with the eye of one who was looking for something to complete a game.

Standing up, she roamed over to the trunks, an old one that she was familiar with and one newly placed. "I know what's in this trunk...it's the dresses and gowns and undergarments from Aunt Winnie's tour," she muttered. "So what is in you?"

The newly placed trunk was not pretty like the steamer trunk, with its bright leather straps and its exotic labels from far off ports; places with names that led young girls, or one young girl, to dream of travel and love and adventure. The second trunk seemed of an older vintage, plain, and at first glance, far less interesting. It wasn't nearly as large as the steamer. However, it's humped-backed crown could hold secrets that Winnie hadn't been able to share or perhaps wanted to share. There was a large H~A~B painted in tarnished gold on the face beneath the latch. "Harriet Anne Belfry," Nora guessed aloud.

Nora had seen tin-types of Aunt Harriet…everyone in the family had. She remembered that Granddad John had been rather boorish in his descriptions and memories of his aunt, much to Winnie's chagrin. Both Connie and David had seen the tintype on one of the tables in Granddad's parlor, and had made fun of the old fashioned, rather plain woman in the picture. Neither had been called on their behavior. Only Nora, who was drawn to the tin-type, had been curtly told not to touch the frame, as it was an antique and very valuable. So she was relegated to looking without touching.

Still, she'd seen enough to judge the woman in the picture as no one's fool. While her garments were not the style that Connie and David were used to, she was stylish, if plain, dressed for her times. Nora could only guess at what things in life the woman had left for Winnie to treasure besides the cottage at Misty Hollow. Harriet had been the first Belfry to live at the Hollows. The basic design of the house, the placement of its foundation, had been her doing.

She knelt down beside the trunk and studied the latch and lock. If it were locked, she'd need to find the key. Touching the latch, she found the trunk wasn't locked and was easy enough to open. Inside, she found a diary on top—Harriet's diary—and a box containing Harriet's most treasured trinkets and personal jewelry. Beneath were amazing garments that were wrapped in tissue paper that felt like velvet instead of brittle paper fibers. It was as fresh as it was the day it had been packed, and smelled of sweet cinnamon potpourri in a sachet that was still soft and pliable. It amazed Nora, reaching in, that the fabrics were as vibrant in hue and soft to the touch as they had been one hundred years or more before. Soft gauzy dressing gowns, evening dresses, and day dresses that had been lovingly stored. Even soft kidd slippers to match were in the trunk, all looking familiar and comforting, even though Nora had never seen them.

She carefully unlatched the lid compartments. They were three distinctive partitioned areas. The center was the largest, and contained a very beautiful and very ornate mirror, brush, and comb set with the finest silver, shell, and bone. The back of the mirror sported an H for Harriet, and the brush bristles were very fine and still quite supple. The bone of the teeth in the comb looked as if it had been carefully used, and amazingly, not one was missing. Her fingers touched the handle of the mirror with reverence; she'd always wanted a set like this, ever since she'd seen the one that Aunt Mary Kate had given Connie when Connie turned sixteen. But she hadn't even bothered to ask for one, as she knew it was very costly. Connie had seen to her knowing how much the set cost when she yanked the brush out of Nora's hand after showing the set off to the younger girl. She had a feeling that Great Grand Aunt Harriet would have been gentler.

Returning the set to its hiding place, Nora opened the compartment on the right side. She was delighted to find it full of hankies and gloves and silk stockings. In the last compartment Nora found tin-types of a woman and a young

girl. Turning the old image over, she read an inscription...
Aunt Agatha and Harriet. There were several photos of
the pair, and some of Agatha alone at various stages of her
life. Nora noted the remarkable resemblance she bore to the
woman Agatha. Then another tintype caught her attention.
Agatha and an old man who was clearly a Native American.
They were seated, in deep discussion, oblivious to the person
who took this shot. They were seated in the spot where the
garden wall now stood. Turning the tintype over, Nora read...
Agatha and Mketashshekakah...Black Hawk. It was dated 1866.

Under the tin-types were letters from Agatha to her niece
Harriet. They were warm, genuinely generous letters that
spoke of a special bond. Reading them gave Nora a feeling
of inclusiveness, of being part of something bigger. Agatha's
handwriting was beautiful and very clear, and her tone in the
letter was understanding and gentle...much like Winnie had
been with Nora. Under all the letters, notes, and cards was a
leather book. Nora opened it...the first page read the Official
Diary, and under the title was the name Agatha Belfry and
the year 1865.

Nora's hands shook; the thoughts of the first person to
own this property were in her hands. She wondered if this
was what Aunt Winnie had wanted her to find. Could this
hold the key to help her make a full transition? Would it help
her find the means to control the power she was going to need
to harness to defeat Garnel?

Winnie had told her that it was Aunt Agatha who had
bought this land, with her own money. However, there was
little else that she had said about her. Nora had seen the tin-
types in the collection of family portraits in the Belfry Estate

House. She knew later shots of Aunt Agatha, but the shot from 1865 was something she'd never seen before. She wondered who had taken it. She looked at Agatha's handwriting; it was strong, clean, clear. The book opened to a page and Nora read.

April 15, 1865
Mother has taken to her bed. The assassination of Mr. Lincoln was more than she could abide. I have been chosen to accompany Mother to the funeral. My own travel plans are postponed.

Nora moved forward in the diary.

July 10, 1865
Mother and I are to accompany Julia Wilkerson and her mother on a canal cruise. Julia's doctor feels that she needs to be out of the city for the rest of her confinement. Her mother, Mrs. O'Connor, will also be abroad. Father and I hope this is just the thing to help mother out of her depression.

July 18, 1865
Sitting on the deck of the Wilkerson yacht with Julia. She is so excited about the coming blessed event. I've never seen her so happy or so beautiful. When we are alone, outside our mother's hearing, Julia and I discuss the women's right to vote movement. Mother and Mrs. O'Conner have been consoling one another. This trip seems to be doing both of them a world of good. Julia supports my refusal of Mr. Gray.

July 20, 1865
Took a carriage ride ashore, just Julia and I. She wanted to

show me the land Daniel, her husband, has purchased for a summer house to be built. The land out there is very reasonably priced, and so beautiful. Julia thinks I should also purchase a bit of land and build a summer place of my own. Now, I must convince my father.

September 3, 1865
Father and I went out to look at a parcel of land not too far down the country road from where Daniel and Julia are going to build. The parcel is lovely, with a stream and a pond. It is heaven outside the city. Father is going to help me get the best price for it. He called me a ban-draoidh; he said I was very much like his grandmother in the old country. Sometimes my father is very difficult to read. I thought he was going to give me more than a bit of trouble over the land. To my utter surprise, he not only agreed to the purchase, but insisted upon seeing it firsthand. He sees what I do, and the need for me to be there.

September 28, 1865
In the past three weeks, I have made the journey out to the parcel of land several times. The fates wanted me to be there, of this I am sure. I met the man that Father and I both saw wandering about. He says his name is Mketashshekakah...it means Black Hawk. He is very old, and I told Father, who believes he is a wind walker. Black Hawk said he saw me in a dream before I came to look at the parcel. He says his dreams are true. He was surprised when I told him I've seen him before. He told me that his tribe has called the land I purchased Misty Hollow. I'm having the name registered.

Nora stopped reading. Winnie had never told her where the name Misty Hollow had come from. Nor had she ever mentioned the old Indian, Black Hawk. With as many things as Winnie had told her, she was finding there were important facts Winnie had left out. She looked at the diary, and had an idea that Winnie had found a loophole in her agreement with the Garnel. This was Agatha's story, not Winnie's. And it was in Agatha's own hand that Nora was learning the origins. Winnie's life started much later.

She opened to another page. "Teach me what I need to know, Aunt Agatha!" Her index finger moved down the page. "Tell me about Garnel."

October 10, 1865
Spent this past week camped out at Misty Hollow. Black Hawk agrees with Father that we should hold off on building a house for now. He told me he is a Guardian, and he keeps a creature bound within the Hollow. He called the creature a Windigo, but intimated that it is unlike any his people have ever encountered. He says that his time on Earth is coming to an end, and that I am to be his replacement. I would be lying if I said this doesn't trouble me. However, I admit I agree with him. I am drawn to Misty Hollow, like a moth to a flame.

October 11, 1865
After a long discussion with Father, I find that I'm in agreement that the creature that Black Hawk's people trapped and have kept bound isn't a Windigo after all. Father listened to my second hand descriptions, and said it sounded more like a creature that Celts battled back home in the Highlands. Father called it a Garnel, and had a description of one such creature in one of his books. Father also told me his grandmother did battle with one. He mused, it must

run in the blood. He said that the elders of our clan had tried to give instruction to Great Grandmother, trying to control her. She listened to what they had to say; however, when the time came to do battle, she did as she felt was right. Father said he believes that kind of strength is also in me.

October 28, 1865
I write this from my tent, on the hillside of Misty Hollow. Black Hawk insisted that I needed to be here when October 31st comes. There is much more activity down in the swamp. That thing cries out like what my Irish grandmother calls a Banshee. It's enough to curdle one's blood. I asked Black Hawk why his people chose this spot to trap the creature. He told me that I must learn to look closer at this place. I didn't know what he meant until this evening at sunset. It was then that I saw the glow. It dances along the rocks, going up and down the hillside. When I told Black Hawk what I saw, he said the creature cannot pass through the glow. He also showed me how he reinforces the glow. I was not surprised; what that old man did was to set wards. Something both my grandmothers taught me to do long ago.

October 30, 1865
I have learned so much in this week. We are ready to face the Garnel together. Black Hawk is a good teacher. I will miss him when he is gone. However, he says the Great Father in the Sky has chosen wisely. I know he was disappointed that it wasn't a male warrior to take his place. Even though he does not say it, I know it is true. I fear this shall be the last battle for Black Hawk. I pray that I have learned enough in this short time to do honor to the title Guardian.

> *November 1, 1865*
> *Last night's battle was far more difficult than I had imagined it would be. It took so much energy out of poor old Black Hawk, but together we prevented that thing from getting loose. We have sent it into hibernation for at least another year. Black Hawk said last night he hoped I would learn how to lengthen the time of its hibernation. He said before he left me last night that I had learned from him all he had to teach me. That I was going to have to learn the rest on my own, as each Guardian needs to do. He looked so tired, so drained. This morning I found him in his little cave...he had passed in the night. He went peacefully...his face was calm, and almost serene. I will have him buried here at the Hollow.*

Nora closed the diary, feeling she'd learned what she needed to face this day. Returning the items to the compartment, Nora gently fitted things back into the Camelback and closed the trunk. She wondered how Winnie had gotten this heavy trunk up here and where she'd had it before moving it to the secret room. As far as Nora knew, the only entry was that one door that went down to Winnie's room. More mysteries to solve later. For now, she had learned something that was important, if only to her. The sun was coming up, and soft rays began to peek into the window.

Feeling a bit more tranquil and ready to face whatever was coming, Nora exited the sanctuary and returned to her own room. She bathed, dressed, and prepared to join the others when something caused her to pause. She had the impending feeling that trouble was on its way. "Connie," she muttered. "Why can't that troublemaker just leave it alone?" The impression became stronger, and Nora guessed that

Connie wasn't coming alone.

Rushing down to the kitchen, she shouted, "Incoming!" and prayed that her house guests would know that meant trouble.

~*~

Daniel McGowan stared at Connie. "I thought you said the cottage was a hovel."

"Compared to the way I live, it is," she said firmly.

"Constance, this is an American Crafts style cottage." His voice dripped disdain. "No wonder Nora is reluctant to sell. The place must be stunning inside; look at that profile." He seemed impressed by his first viewing of the inherited cottage, and that didn't make Connie happy. "I wonder who the architect was."

"Look again! It's a mausoleum, and a monstrosity," Connie glowered. "It's not some shrine to great architecture. Remember why we are here." She pulled on the parking brake before shutting off the car. Turning to her handsome passenger, she narrowed her eyes. "If you want a piece of that nice fat commission, you'd better get on board and help me get that twit to sign the papers."

Daniel yawned. "Connie, you don't frighten me, so can the hostility. I'm already a partner in the firm…unlike you."

"I'm sure that Euro trash boyfriend of hers is trying to milk her for all she's worth."

Daniel sighed. "Sounds like you're mad…or worse, *jealous*," he teased. "Because someone possibly beat you to the milking." He held up his perfectly manicured hand. "Don't worry, I know the drill…and dear little Nora was always putty in my hands."

"See that she still is," Connie snarled, "Or there'll be no pot of gold at the end of the rainbow."

~*~

Nora pulled the shawl that had been Winnie's about her as she moved to the front porch. "Don't bother, Connie; the Hollow is not for sale," she said loudly as her cousin exited her car. "Just get right back in that fancy car of yours and leave."

"I've brought someone to see you," Connie answered, ignoring Nora's attempt at putting her off. "Don't be so rude."

Nora braced herself. She could feel Liam and Robyn watching from the house; Byntwig had taken refuge in the cold cellar, and would be monitoring from there. "You're not welcome," she said firmly.

Daniel leaned on the car. "Hello, baby," he said in a voice that could have enticed nuns to do dirty things. "Miss me?"

"Like a toothache," she said, finding it easy to voice the dissatisfaction she'd felt for several years now. Harboring secrets had left her bitter. But knowledge of who and what Daniel was had given her power. At the moment, he was as smarmy as the creature in the swamp. Neither had the least bit of allure.

The man in the dark wool overcoat chuckled. "Why Nora, did you go and find a sense of humor?"

"I've found many things since you've been out of my life, McGowan; humor, respect, independence." She glared at him. "Take your pick." She kept her body rigid, not allowing them to think she would soften.

Daniel looked over at Connie to gauge her reaction, then when he turned back to Nora he played the concerned ex-lover. "Connie tells me you're seeing someone who's… questionable. I just want to make sure you're not being taken advantage of, baby."

"How would either of you know what's questionable?" Nora laughed. "You want to talk about my having been taken advantage of? Connie was married, and you were engaged to me. Didn't stop you two from having a torrid affair under everybody's nose, leaving me to look the complete fool and shoulder all the blame for the breakup."

Connie's face turned crimson with anger. "Nora, you're turning this to favor you—"

"No!" Nora said determinedly. "I'm stating the *truth*; you two snakes are a pair of cheats. Now you're trying to cheat me out of my inheritance, and whatever happiness I've found in life." She looked at Daniel without feeling the racy heart he used to give her. "Get off my property before I call the county sheriff to haul you off for trespassing."

"Nora, I'm concerned for you," he said, as if they were still on speaking terms. "A rebound romance…."

"Oh, don't give me that crap." Nora placed her hands on the rail in front of her. "What rebound? You and I broke up years ago! You don't care about me, and neither does my *loving* cousin. The only thing you two ever cared about was dollar signs. Now kindly leave before I call the sheriff's office."

Nora knew that if she gave a signal Liam would come out. She wanted to handle this herself, however. In the back of her mind she had a feeling that was the best way to go about it. After all, once she was The Guardian of Misty Hollow, Liam, Robyn, and Byntwig would all return to wherever it was they came from. Depending on a man that wasn't going to be there would not be smart. Not now, not in the future. Nora experienced a surge of pride and the rush of confidence race in her blood. She could do this! Winnie was right, she was up to this, and any other battle.

Daniel moved forward. "You're not going to call the sheriff…," he said, trying to smooth her ruffled feathers.

Nora reached into her pocket, hit a button, and waited until the operator at the sheriff's office answered. "Yes, this is Nora Belfry at Misty Hollow; I've got some unwelcome guests who refuse to leave."

Backing off quickly, Daniel opened the car door. "It's not worth problems with cops," he warned Connie. "I can't be involved in a legal dispute, not over this."

Connie too moved to the car. "You haven't heard the last of this, Nora."

As the car pulled back down the drive, Nora turned her attentions to the sheriff's operator. "Millie, you were right, that did the trick. Tell Sheriff Miller I'm grateful for the advice. I'll call again if there's really trouble, thanks." She disconnected and smiled. She slipped the cell phone back into her pocket and watched her cousin pulling out of her drive with a deeper satisfaction than she'd ever felt.

Just as she was about to turn and go back in the house, she became aware of more trouble. Connie had stopped the car on the curb of the road outside the drive. "What are you up to now?" she whispered.

Chapter 12

Connie stopped the car when they were far enough out of the drive that she felt they couldn't be seen. "That self-righteous, ungrateful little bitch," she snapped viciously. "Who the hell does she think she is?"

Daniel gave her an amused smirk. "You have to admit, Connie, she had us pegged." He was amused even if Connie wasn't. "Who'd have thought *she* had the guts to tell us off?"

"Oh, really," she growled. "If it wasn't for me, she'd never have been engaged at all! You really think any man gave her a look before I introduced her to you?"

The man in the dark overcoat cocked a brow upward. "When, may I ask, did she grow a pair?" He had never seen Nora quite so in control. "Had she been so spirited I might have spent a bit more time getting to know her. Who knew she had balls?"

"Call the cops on me, will she? Turn down the generous offer for that hovel? Well, now I'll see to it she gets nothing!"

The woman seated in the driver's seat glared. "She has no idea of what she's brought down on herself." She picked up her cell phone and dialed. "Yes, I'd like to speak to Mr. Brenan, its Constance Logan calling.... I want to contest a will."

~*~

Dark eyes watched from a short distance, and an evil grin spread on the face of the Garnel. He had felt the energy of this one before, and knew she was open to his suggestions.

~*~

Liam came out to the porch. "You didn't have to stand against them alone." His voice sounded a bit hurt. "I could have helped."

Nora turned to look at him. "Are you going to be here after I've faced Garnel?"

"No," he answered quietly, a bit reluctantly, but with finality. "But, Nora, I'm here now."

She shook her head and pulled her shawl tighter. "Robyn and Byntwig won't be here either," she said stubbornly. "I have to learn to stand up for myself, on my own. This seemed as good a time as any to start. And I find I like it." Her soft green eyes looked away from him. She hated that he could make her pulse race without even trying. "I appreciate that you would want to help, but I can't keep leaning on and depending on you to save me, Liam. You're not going to be here after. I don't want to form a dependence I can't count on."

The Celt leaned on one of the posts that held up the roof of the porch. "What you say has merit," he agreed. "You do need to stand on your own. It's just that saving you is rather pleasant, and has most pleasant rewards."

Nora blushed. "Thank you, kind sir."

He reached out a hand to touch her sleeve. "Who was that man?"

"That was the man I was engaged to," Nora whispered. "While engaged to me, he and Connie were carrying on an affair. They used me to cover things up so Connie's husband wouldn't suspect anything." She shook off the old hurt. "His name is Daniel McGowan, and he and Connie work for the same realtor agency."

"Are they still...?" He paused, wishing to be delicate.

"No, I don't think so," Nora said. "That ended about the same time Connie's marriage did, as far as I know. But they still work in the same realtor office." She pulled the shawl tighter. "It's getting cold out here...maybe we should go in. I've got work to do."

~*~

Byntwig sensed that Nora was preoccupied. Her concentration was not what it should be, and her ability to follow his directions seemed hampered. "What is it that has you lost in thought?" he asked.

"Connie," Nora answered. "I've never seen her so... driven." She set aside the parchment paper that she had been working on. "Byntwig, it's as if she were being...*pushed*." Nora knew her cousin, and knew what usually drove her on. "She has always been an overachiever when it comes to most things in her life, be it school or the real estate business. I mean, I know she's damned good at what she does, but she's never gone after anything the way she's going after me and the Hollow. She's had papers drawn up for the sale of this place since before Aunt Winnie was even cold, from what my sources tell me."

The old troll pulled his beard as he listened. "You said that she hates this place; any idea of why?"

"I don't know." Nora leaned back in the chair and looked about the cozy room. "Maybe I idealize this place. To me, it's *home*...always has been. I loved coming here as a child, and even in my teen years. Once I went to college it was harder to get away. I took courses all year long, and didn't get summers off like I did before. My first year in college I lived on campus, but for the last years, I moved back home before my folks left. I used to come out here for weekends back then, and Winnie and I would hike up and down the moraine like we did when I was a little kid." She smiled at the memory of Winnie in her khakis, marching up and down, pointing to plants or birds and expecting Nora to recall their names. "Back when it was Connie, David, and I spending time here, we did all sorts of nature walks and woodland crafts...swimming in the creek, watching the cranes and the other migratory birds nest, making reed baskets, fishing...."

"I can see how happy this makes you," Byntwig chuckled. "However, think back; did your cousins seem happy as well?"

"I thought so," Nora confessed. "But looking back...," she bit her lower lip. "No...they seemed to be just going through the motions. Connie was never the outdoorsy type. When she got into her teens, she would make up excuses for not doing the hikes. David was a toady, then and now, and he'd follow Connie's lead. I was amazed he got through law school without her. But even when Aunt Winnie would take us to the stables up the road they would make a fuss." She sighed deeply. "Connie didn't like the smell of the stables, or the quality of horseflesh…there was always something she didn't like."

"Tell me about how they behaved when they reached puberty." Byntwig had a thoughtful look on his face, as if he'd just thought of something that was elemental.

"Connie turned fourteen the year I turned ten, and David was twelve." Nora thought back to that summer. "Aunt Winnie told me that we had to be more thoughtful of Connie, that there would be days she'd be out of sorts. I know now that she meant that Connie had come into having cycles, but I didn't know it then." Nora closed her eyes. "Connie seemed more edgy, and less cooperative than usual. I remember she pitched a fit about having to be at the Hollow."

"Was that before or after she arrived?"

"After," Nora said, opening her eyes. "She was sulking on the ride over here. We came in one car with her mother, Aunt Mary Kate, driving. Connie was huddled in the back seat next to the door…I was in the middle, and David huddled by the other door. It was as if they couldn't put enough space between us." Nora's eyes widened. "Wait a minute," she said urgently. "I remember something. Connie got really mean the moment we crossed the gateway and started up the drive." She looked over at the troll. "The Garnel?" She leaned forward. "Do you think the Garnel had some kind of effect on her?"

"It's in hibernation most of the year," Byntwig explained with a grimace. "Yet even in hibernation, it can stimulate and provoke, or even prompt susceptible subjects to its will. Subjects with dark hearts are always what it feeds upon."

"No wonder Winnie didn't force Connie to go hiking," Nora replied. "She must have known that Connie was vulnerable." A new thought worried her. "Why wasn't I?"

"Because you were more than just a potential candidate for the Guardian," Byntwig snickered. "Although anyone in the bloodline is a potential, few actually have the calling awaken in them. Those that do seem to have a bit more imperviousness built in at an early age. It lessens in some and strengthens in others. There's no why or wherefore…it is what it is."

"That's not much of a help." Nora crossed her arms as she leaned back. "So no one knows why some have more resistance to the Garnel than others?"

"No," he sighed.

"Tell me again why Winnie couldn't train me," Nora inquired.

"Winnie forgot to be on her guard," he cautioned. "And she was prideful."

"I don't have that," Nora sighed. "I never had reason to be prideful…Connie saw to reminding me of that fact for as long as I can remember."

Byntwig seemed amused. "Those early years, when you were constantly being torn down by Connie and this David, made you stronger. Winnie saw it and used it. What she couldn't train you to know, she let them."

"I've never looked at it that way."

The troll snickered. "Want to hide a weapon, put it in plain sight." He pulled his beard again. "Your cousin has been out here twice now trying to get you to sell, and the Garnel is awake. This is his doing."

Nora shook her head. "Connie had the papers ready to go at the reading of the will. That was before I moved in, before it awakened."

"As I said, it hibernates, but it is still active and dangerous," warned the old troll. "And with Winnie dying, it must have awakened early."

"And my digging my feet in must piss it off."

~*~

Nora received a call that evening from Benton. "My dear, there's been a petition brought forth against the will."

"Connie?"

"Yes, how did you know?"

Nora rolled her eyes. "Oh, it just figures. She's been out here twice trying to get me to sign my inheritance away. Is there any way to stop her?"

Benton was silent for a moment, but Nora could hear papers being shifted. "There may be," he said at last. "But it will mean you taking a bond out on her."

"Do it," Nora said. "She can't freeze my accounts, can she?"

"No," Benton informed the young woman. "Winnie had those in trust for you since you were sixteen."

"Good. The less disruption to my routine now, the better," Nora stated.

"I can set up a judge's chamber meeting with all parties," Benton said. "On Monday morning."

"All parties?"

"The petition cites David and their mother, as well as your Uncle John and your cousin Jack."

"I doubt Aunt Mary Kate has any idea of what dear Connie is up to," grumbled a very unhappy Nora. "Set it up… I'll be there with bells on." Hanging up, she heard the howl in the darkness outside. "I hope Winnie was smart enough to put up protections. If not...God help us all." She tapped her chin. "I wonder how one sets a ward up? Maybe it's time for this Belfry witch to learn."

Nora didn't sit in the parlor with her companions that evening. She went up to the hidden room in the attic. Picking up Aunt Agatha's diary, she read carefully what she had written about her first Samhain here at the Hollow. The night that Black Hawk passed after strengthening the wards.

Peering out the window, looking down at the garden wall, she saw something that had always been there, just out of her sight. The flow of energy in the wall. Nora smiled. It would hold. She wasn't ready to try and augment it, for fear of causing it to fall.

Chapter 13

Benton was in the hall outside the chamber when Nora arrived, and he looked worried. He approached Nora swiftly. "Your cousins and their lawyer are in there already. What kept you?"

"Car trouble," she murmured. "I had to use Tin Lizzy to get here. Someone snuck into the garage last night and put something in my VW's gas tank." She placed a hand to his sleeve before they entered. "You said my cousins are here; what about Aunt Mary Kate?"

"She's a no show so far," Benton said. "John and Jack are not here either."

"Give me a moment." Nora took out her phone and speed dialed her aunt's number. "Aunt Mary Kate, are you all right?"

"I'm fine, Nora. How nice to hear your voice."

"Where are you?" she asked quietly. There were noises in the background she couldn't identify.

"I'm in Florida. I have my annual golf outing." Her aunt's voice sounded pleased.

"Oh," Nora winced. "I forgot about that...."

"Nora," her aunt's tone went from happy to concern in a heartbeat. "Has something happened?"

"David and Connie are contesting the will, and have named you as a plaintiff as well. They've dragged Uncle John and Jack in to boot," she said, knowing this was no time to shelter her aunt. "We're having a meeting with a judge in about five minutes, but you're not here and neither is Uncle John. I'm wondering if he was even notified."

The line was quiet for a moment. "Is Benton there with you?" she asked tersely.

"Yes, ma'am."

"Put him on," her aunt commanded.

Nora motioned the lawyer to take her phone and she stepped back. He listened, made a comment, and nodded vigorously. Nora bit her lower lip, trying to remain positive. She watched as the lawyer who had worked for Winnie began to grin like a Cheshire cat, and she prayed it was a good sign.

When he closed the phone, she asked, "Well?"

"In good time," Benton assured her. He motioned toward the judge's door.

When they entered the outer office of the chamber, the secretary nodded and showed them into the chamber. Connie, dressed for success in a red Chanel power suit, preened and smiled at Nora, who was dressed more conservatively in black and white. David sat at his sister's side and smirked.

Brenan stood up and offered his hand politely to his opponent Benton. "Good to see you again," he said cordially.

"And you," Benton responded. "I see Judge Mattson is running late."

"As usual," the other jested. "We could save him the trouble; all you have to do is have your client sign these papers."

"Not a chance," Benton said. He then directed Nora to take a seat across the aisle from Connie.

"You're going to lose," Connie taunted threateningly. "I always win."

"Not this time," Nora sighed, and settled in the chair.

Judge Robert Mattson entered the chamber, his robes still on since he had left court a few moments before. "I apologize for my tardiness," he said, moving to his desk. "But that's the chance you take when you ask for a judicial hearing." He took his seat and addressed the lawyers. "Benton, Brenan, let us begin."

Brenan nodded. "I represent the Logan family and members of the Belfry family, who are contesting the will of one Winifred Belfry."

"I object," Benton said with a smug grin.

"To what?" the judge asked.

"My honorable opponent is mistaken," Benton answered. "He does not represent the Logan family."

"Of course I do," Brenan protested.

"Well, not all of the Logan family, that is," Benton corrected. "As I happen to represent Mrs. Logan, the mother of his clients."

Judge Mattson watched Brenan's face fall. "Interesting." He made a note.

"What?" Connie bellowed. "Since when?"

"It seems Miss Logan here took it upon herself to make her mother a party to this, without her mother's knowledge or consent. Mrs. Logan is in Florida, but has asked that it be made clear that the will is fine with her as it stands." Benton continued over Connie's protests. "I have my doubts as to my colleague representing the interests of John Belfry and his son. As they are not here, we cannot ask them."

"You told her?" Connie demanded.

"Of course," Benton acknowledged. "She is named as a party to the challenge. I had questions for her."

Connie blanched. "Damn."

Brenan turned to his client. "She didn't know?" Connie glared at him.

David groaned, seeing trouble headed for him and his sister, not just with the court but with their mother. "Connie," he whined. "You said everything was set."

"So who is actually challenging the will?" Mattson asked with a grin.

"I am, and my brother," Connie said tightly. "It's not fair to anyone in the family."

"May I see a copy of the will?" Mattson asked Benton.

Nora remained content to quietly watch this play out and remain still. She began to see how being perceived as mousy and ineffectual could play in her favor.

The judge read over the will. "The other beneficiaries, do they have any complaints?"

"Not to my knowledge," Benton answered. "In fact, this is the list of those who were present for the reading." He handed a page to the judge. "And the recorded minutes of the reading. Mr. John Belfry the second and his son John the third were not present for the reading, and haven't issued any complaints. They accepted their inheritances and have made no complaints as to content. As far as I know, John Belfry the second is not even aware that his niece has brought this complaint."

Brenan looked surprised when Benton handed him a copy as well.

Sitting quietly, her hands in her lap, Nora gauged the judge's reactions. He was amused, Brenan was unsettled, and Connie was pissed. David...well, David was David. She kept her own feelings and facial expression to herself. Once her eyes met with those of the judge; she didn't glance away, but she didn't give him defiance either.

"Miss Logan, just what is it you found unfair?" he challenged Connie.

"It isn't equitable," she said firmly. "The property should be sold, as well as the contents of the cottage, and the proceeds should be equally distributed between *all* the heirs."

"I see." The judge folded his hands over the papers on his desk. "Was that how it was when John Belfry the first died?"

Connie's eyes narrowed, but she answered as politely as her temper would allow. "I'm not sure I understand the question."

"Do you feel the will of John Belfry was equitable?"

"It's not the same thing," Connie blinked. "Granddad John had a son, a direct heir—"

"Did he leave all his grandchildren the exact same amounts?"

"I have no idea," Connie frowned.

"I'm not sure I believe you," Judge Mattson stated coldly.

"As you were present for the reading of this will, you are aware that your great aunt thought her brother's will favored some over others."

Connie's jaw tightened.

Mattson went on. "Have you asked your Uncle John Belfry if he objects, or your cousin John?"

"No," Connie answered. "I thought I'd save them the trouble."

"Did you?"

Nora didn't think that Mattson sounded amused anymore, and she wondered if he had some connection to the family that she was unaware of. The hair on the nape of her neck began to prickle, and she had a feeling that Connie was about to become toast.

"Why do you object to Miss Belfry being awarded this property?"

Connie's hand clenched the arm of the chair she was seated in. "As I said, it was inequitable."

"Is there any other reason?" Mattson inquired.

"Isn't that reason enough?" Connie challenged rudely. "Really?"

David placed a hand to his forehead. "Connie…," he warned.

Their lawyer cleared his throat. "Judge, it does seem odd that Miss Belfry has been left all this…property, when the other heirs were given far less."

"How much time did you spend with your great aunt?" The judge was writing again and not looking at Connie.

"We spent summers with her."

"When?" The judge jotted down notes.

Connie blinked, and seemed reluctant to answer. "When we were adolescents."

"And you, Miss Belfry?"

"I spent summers with Aunt Winnie as well," she answered truthfully.

Connie preened again, thinking she had tipped the balance.

Mattson looked at both women. "And after your adolescence?"

The woman in red went rigid. "I went to work when I was sixteen, and then I went away to college. There was little time for frittering away my time. I'm sure Aunt Winnie understood." She began to tap a toe impatiently. "I saw her at the usual family gatherings and holidays."

"And you, miss?" The judge turned to Nora.

"I spent more time with her, I suppose. I didn't go away to school like Connie or David. I went to the local college and I lived closer. I used to come out for the odd weekends, and spent my holiday vacations with Winnie after my parents moved west due to my father's health issues."

Again the judge made a note, and Nora saw Connie's face harden.

Mattson turned to Connie. "What do you stand to gain by forcing your cousin to liquidate her inheritance?"

Connie's jaw dropped.

Brenan glanced at Connie. "You have nothing to gain, do you?"

Connie refused to answer.

The judge turned to Nora. "What does she stand to gain?"

"Besides a very healthy commission on the sale of the

property? Power and status in her company," Nora answered honestly. "And a partnership she's lusted after for the last eight years."

David scrunched down in his chair, looking like he was wishing he could disappear.

Mattson tapped his fingers on the desk. "Miss Logan, I see no reason to allow the challenge of the Winifred Belfry will. None of the other heirs seem to be worried about Miss Belfry here inheriting the Hollow. Your own mother does not challenge the distribution of the estate of her aunt." He made one more note on the legal paper. "I do question your ethics," he informed the lady in red. "Request denied." He looked at Brenan. "I'd advise you to get all your facts from now on."

"Yes, sir."

Mattson looked at Nora. "I wish you well, Miss Belfry."

Nora stood up with poise she'd never felt before. "Thank you, sir." She smiled softly and shook his hand. Turning, she heard Connie gnash her teeth.

Chapter 14

Nora drove to the little garage that Aunt Winnie had used for all her automotive needs just outside Hickory Hills…it had been there for years. Jake had towed her VW over to the shop and was going over it. She parked Tin Lizzy and walked to the open bay door of the garage; she could hear Jake's cursing and took her time. Once in the bay, she called, "Jake, it's Nora Belfry."

Jake was about her father's age, and Winnie had sworn by his expertise. He had owned this shop for as long as Nora could remember, having inherited the business from his father. Dressed in greasy overalls that were well worn, he came out from under the lift, wiped his hands on a cloth hanging off one pocket, and moved to Nora and the open door. "Miss Belfry." He nodded to her.

"Nora, please," she said.

"Nora it is then." He gave her a toothy if lopsided grin. "You were right; someone's put pepper in the gas tank. I'm surprised you saw it."

Nora shook her head in disgust. "Is this going to be expensive?"

"It would have been if you had run the engine," he told her. "It's more time consuming than expensive. I have to drain and purge the entire system, and steam the tank clean, filter the gas, and recycle the fuel."

"Still sounds like it's going to be expensive," she mused. "About how long will the VW be in the shop?"

"I'll have her back to you on November the first," he promised. "And since your aunt had a long time account with us, I'm going to give you the same rate I'd give her. I'm hoping you'll stay with us for both vehicles."

"I wouldn't trust anyone else with Tin Lizzy, or with my little Bug," Nora assured him. "Aunt Winnie swore by you, and having driven the old girl," she motioned to the vintage car she'd arrived in, "I can see the caliber of service you provide. I'm hooked, Jake."

Jake's grin widened. "That's good to hear." He gave her a wink. "Now you just go along, and I'll have your little Bug fixed and running like a champ."

"Thank you, Jake." She bade him goodbye.

~*~

When Nora arrived home both Robyn and Liam were seated on the porch awaiting her arrival. When she parked the auto they were just outside the garage.

"Did you win?" Robyn inquired.

"Yes," Nora said.

Liam crossed his arms. "You don't seem as pleased as I would have expected."

"I'm concerned," Nora admitted. "I think Garnel has Connie doing his dirty work."

"Byntwig thinks so too," Robyn chimed in, sounding a bit like a tattletale.

Nora looked at the garage; nothing in this section had been disturbed. Only the carport had been open to attack. But that didn't mean the culprit wouldn't try again. Nora had a feeling that, after Connie being told in the judge's chambers that she didn't have a case, another assault was inevitable. She didn't wish to chance it or chance damages to Tin Lizzy, but she didn't trust her own abilities just yet. "I need to talk to Byntwig," she said quietly. "Alone."

She could feel that she was being watched, and that the eyes on her were not human. Winnie's wards on the wall were holding, but only just. Soon, what she'd done to protect the property and the house would be diminished to the point that it would not hold the Garnel back. She didn't have time to worry about what the next few days would bring as far as the creature was concerned. She had humans she needed to keep from creating havoc.

Byntwig was setting up in the parlor. For the first time Nora noticed the design on the huge Oriental rug that covered the hardwood floor. It was a very large five pointed star that had an ivy vine wound about it, inside a large ivy and oak circle. The old troll looked up from his task and nodded to her. "Give me a few moments, child," he warned.

"Take your time," she said, watching from the archway in the foyer. He nodded again and went back to his task. His knowledge was far reaching, and she envied him. He had the benefit of having been raised to be a mage; he hadn't had to cram a lifetime of learning into a short eight week period. In his world, he was accepted for what he was.

Moving to the center of the star, he raised his arms and began to chant in a tongue that was strange to Nora's ears, but rather musical in its own right. Having become accustomed to the vibrations of the house and the energies that flowed through Misty Hollow, Nora could feel the change in the protective wards. This was old power…this was old knowledge. It felt good. It felt right.

Byntwig lowered his arms and turned to her. "I do hope you don't mind reinforcements."

"Not at all," she said. "I was going to ask for your help." She looked out toward the garage. "It was pepper in the gas tank. It could have destroyed my car; as it is, it's going to be a costly fix."

"Had you not noticed the gas tank cover being ajar," Byntwig replied, "it could have been much worse. It could have cost your life."

"I'm just lucky whoever did it didn't get into the garage and ruin Tin Lizzy." Nora took a step into the circle. "Whoever did this has no regard for personal property." She experienced a surge of electrical energy surrounding her. "The next attack might be on the house itself, or on me."

"Garnel is trying to break you down," the old troll mused. "He is trying to fix it so that you would be more or less helpless against him."

"But I'm not. Am I?"

"Not quite as much as he had hoped," the old troll chuckled darkly. "You are not what you appear to be; that is in your favor."

Allowing the positive flow of cosmic energy to flow through, around, and over her, Nora hoped he was right. "I still can't do what a fully-fledged Guardian, or even a novice mage could do," she admitted. "I've got that working against me."

"You will have to trust your instincts," Byntwig decreed. His old amber eyes danced merrily as he watched her absorb the energy. "But for now, Garnel will only see that you are floundering, and that I have raised the protective wards."

"What about the carriage house?"

"We will have to risk it," the troll sighed. "Unless you'd care to enlist the help of one of Winnie's little woodland friends."

Nora considered the suggestion. "It would have to be something big enough to scare off an intruder. A squirrel or a woodchuck isn't going to do the job." She was very familiar with all the critters that Aunt Winnie took care of. "But we need something that's not going to do damages round the house or to me."

"Barn owl," the old troll closed his eyes. "No," he thought again. "Deer are too likely to get skittish…we need something that has a primal mind." He pulled his snowy beard. "Something Garnel can't sway."

Nora snapped her fingers. "Coyote?"

"Member of the Canis," the old troll nodded slowly. "But would it be trustworthy?"

"I remember Winnie saying there was a pack in the Hollow," Nora spoke quietly. "They always seemed to keep their distance."

"I'm personally not inclined to trust them," the old troll

grew serious. "They could turn on you if they think they have the upper hand. No, we need something more controllable, more honest."

"There's a flock of geese in the meadow," Nora suggested.

"Geese." The old creature's amber eyes began to glow. "Garnel has no sway over geese." He seemed pleased with the thought. "Yes, and wild geese have a fondness for mortals.... Yes." He pulled longer, more even strokes thoughtfully at his beard.

"I don't know...the males in that flock seem awfully aggressive," Nora cautioned. "What about foxes? There's always a den or two in the Hollow."

"Foxes," the old troll's eyes went cold. "Foxes cannot be trusted, ask any wolf."

"Hawks," Nora offered.

"Hawks have promise." He gave her a crooked grin. "What kind of hawks?"

"We have red tailed, and we have peregrines." She gave a wistful smile. "Aunt Winnie was helping in the recovery efforts for the peregrines, and there are several rooks and nests about the place. We were never publicized. Winnie and the wildlife foundation felt it was best not to let too many people know where the birds were. I only know about it because I was helping."

"Peregrines would do very nicely," nodded the old troll. "They bond well to mortals, even when not being kept as hunting birds. Yes," he smiled. "Go, change into some hiking garments. We must be quick in finding you just the right bird." He waved her off. "Go quickly."

~*~

An hour later, the autumn sun was high in the sky. They had still not found just the right bird to satisfy the old troll. Nora was beginning to think that old Byntwig was too picky. He asked questions as they roamed about in an area he proclaimed Garnel free. "Did your cousins know about the hawks and peregrines?"

"Not that I recall," Nora answered as she followed the little man up and down the moraine. "As far as I know Winnie wasn't interested in the recovery program until I was nearly sixteen. By that time David and Connie weren't coming out here anymore. I never told them about the birds, because they weren't interested in discussing anything with me. I doubt that Winnie would have told them either."

"I wish I had met this woman," Byntwig said with a smirk. "She sounds positively cunning."

"I hope you mean that in the nicest way possible," Nora warned. "We're talking about my aunt, remember!"

"I do," he nodded, keeping his eye on something of a trail. "Trolls value cunning and shrewdness and even craftiness as virtues."

"Then you would have adored Winnie," Nora agreed.

He held up his hand and halted quickly. "Listen," he whispered.

Nora went very still and quietly listened. In the distance she could hear the sound that had caught the old troll's ear. Closing her eyes, she listened and smiled. "Peregrines."

"Are you sure?" The troll knew, but wanted to be sure the girl did as well.

"I'd know that cry over any other," she said with a nod. "I love them."

"Come along," he advised. "We've only a few short hours of daylight left, and you must be impressed."

"Impressed?"

"Bonded to a bird," the odd little man snickered. "Once you are, you are considered a part of its flock, and it will protect you and yours as long as it lives."

The hillside was dotted with trees and then gave way to a rocky outcropping that looked rather dangerous; it was there they found the nest. It was situated in such a way that the protected outcropping kept the nest from being blown apart by the winds that could sweep into the Hollow. Peering out were three large peregrines.

"Move forward," Byntwig urged. "Let them get a good look at you."

"What if they don't like me?"

"Move forward!"

Nora looked up at the three birds perched above her, and held her breath as she inched forward. "Nice bird," she said in a wavering voice. "Lovely bird. Pretty bird."

One bird turned away, another hunkered down, but one teetered out of the cave-like area the nest was in and looked at Nora with a cocked head. First it cocked its head one way, then the other, and then it spread its wings and swooped down for a closer look. Nora stood still, and prayed she had not pissed it off. A moment later it landed on some of the rocks not far from her.

Gently and slowly, Nora placed her hand into a leather glove that Byntwig had ordered her to bring along. She then took a piece of raw meat out of a Baggie and offered it to the falcon, which was watching her with interest. It crept forward, looked at her, then the offered treat, and snatched the meat way. It stepped back quickly and gobbled down the treat. Nora didn't bother looking at Byntwig; he'd told her it was imperative that she keep her attention on the bird. She offered a second morsel, and again the bird came toward her slowly. Byntwig had told her to make sure her actions were not jerky, as the bird would take this as a sign of attack. Smoothly she reached out and offered the second treat.

"Very good," Byntwig praised. "You have a natural talent as a falconer."

"If you say so," Nora answered as she watched the bird of prey eat. She took out one more, and this time placed it over the leather glove, and held her hand out to the falcon. It cocked its head, spread its wings, and then rose into the air to land on Nora's outstretched hand. For a moment his eyes and Nora's met before it dipped down to pick up the meat.

"I think he likes you," Byntwig announced.

"He's lovely," Nora said, admiring the handsome bird. "The most magnificent falcon I've seen up close."

The bird stayed on her hand, and she began to speak to it in gentle tones. "I'm Nora; Winnie left the care of the Hollow and its inhabitants to me." The bird gave a soft cry at the mention of her aunt's name. "Yes, I miss her too." Nora sighed. "I need your help," she told the bird, who flapped its wings and stayed hunkered on her hand. "Would you care to nest in the garage at the house? There's a lovely loft like area that has an opening to the open air." The bird settled and Nora began to walk back the way they had come. "You can have your own rook and create your family space there."

~*~

Liam watched as Nora and Byntwig approached with the newest member of the household. "What is this?"

"This is Rex, and he's going to be my watch...." She couldn't call him a dog, it would have been insulting. "Falcon."

"A watch falcon?" Robyn sounded dismissive.

"Yes, and I think he's lovely," Nora said. Byntwig stood back as Nora introduced Rex to his new home. "You are free to come and go; you're neither a pet nor a slave," she told the bird as he left her hand, heading to the opening in the loft. "All I ask is that you don't allow strangers to come onto our land and destroy our property."

The falcon gave a shrill cry, inspected the loft, and hunkered down with its eyes closed.

"Well done," Byntwig praised.

"A watch falcon," muttered the elf. "Nothing if not novel."

With daylight fading, the trio of men and the Guardian in training retreated to the house. There was a cold wind blowing, and both troll and woman were hungry. Nora sat with a steaming mug of soup on the enclosed porch, and watched as Rex began to fill his rookery with straw and wildflowers and other things that would make his nest. She was fascinated. First Rex would bring something up to the enclosed area, and then he'd shove it out if it didn't match up to his expectations.

"He's not behaving like a falcon," Liam observed. "They don't build nests like that."

"He's making a decoy...," Nora said. "That is one smart bird. Anyone seeing the stems over that rail will think it's an owl or some other bird. They'll never know it's a falcon." She watched as the daylight waned.

~*~

Late into the night Nora heard the cries of something less than human. She pulled her blanket tighter about herself. She felt the intrusion before she heard the yelps and rough cuss words hurled at the attacking falcon. A smile came to her lips. "So much for that, Connie," she sighed before going back to sleep, dreaming of riding the wind with her falcon.

~*~

Dark eyes watched as the men sent by the mortal he was using failed in their attack. He shook his head. Was he growing old, or were mortals growing more stupid? He chose the latter. His time was drawing near, and his powers were nearly fully restored. It was only a matter of days and he would utterly destroy the untrained, unprepared young woman. He wouldn't have need of mortals like Constance any longer, and he would happily eliminate her as well. She had disappointed him over and over in the last few weeks, and she would not be worth keeping as a pet.

Garnel moved into the swamp. Being near the decaying plants and dying creatures who had sought refuge here fed him. It was only a matter of days.... He wondered if the mousy little creature would beg for mercy...not that there was any to be had. He almost hoped she would. It would be pleasant to see her crawl after she'd been so arrogant and flippant toward him. He was, after all, a Garnel. "I took down the prideful Winnie, and I'll take you down as well, little mouse," he boasted.

Taking a seat on a dead tree that was hollowed out like a throne, he began to make mental notes of all the horrible things he'd planned, first for the failed Guardian and then for the world. It had been more than two hundred years that he'd been trapped in this Hollow…held first by a native shaman and then by the Guardian. It had been galling, having to watch the human race overrun his world. So many of his kind had fled into the dark mists and dark waters, seeking refuge from the world of man. But he wasn't interested in refuge, he wanted revenge.

His vengeance would begin with the failed Guardian. He planned on making her his example, and then he'd destroy the rest of the human race, one nation at a time, until the world was free of the pests and his kind was free to roam again.

Chapter 15

There were only a few days left, and Nora was beginning to feel the pressure. She still wasn't able to do what Robyn felt she needed to do. She thought that even Byntwig, who tried to be more supportive, had reservations about her skills. She had her own reservations, and was spending more of her private time up in the little sanctuary. Nora felt drawn to the secret space, as if all her answers were up there. She had finished reading Agatha's diary, and letters sent to Agatha by her niece, Anna. She looked through tin-types and familiarized herself with these family members.

Anna had been the one to wear the title Guardian next. Like her aunt before her, she didn't live in the Hollow, but it was Anna who built the little summer house by the pond. It was also Anna who had started the garden wall. She had used stones found on the property, her diary said.

May 1, 1895

Have read the study of the area of Scotland that our family came from. The ban-draoidh used local stones in building ward walls. I think this is something that I need to do. I think Aunt Agatha would approve. Little Harriet spent the weekend here with me. She loved dancing in the meadow this morning to celebrate Mayday. She will make a fine Guardian when her time comes. I fear it will come to her faster than mine came to me. I see visions of death, and I don't think I can keep them at bay. I pray I live long enough to complete the ward wall, and train Harriet.

It meant a great deal to Nora, these snippets of family history...history of the Belfry Guardians at the Hollow. She understood why Winnie couldn't share these things with her. But she wished that she had. She wanted to know these women. These strong, brave Belfry women. They were part of her, and she wanted to make them proud. What struck her was that the family, even the men back before her Grandfather's generation, didn't turn a blind eye. They knew of the magic that was part of the family line. They celebrated it! Until John the first. Nora wondered what it was that had soured John to the magic, and why he treated Aunt Winnie with such disdain.

When she was free to, she was going over Winnie's journals with a fine toothed comb. However, she'd found little of help in the scattered writings thus far. She wondered if it was because she was trying too hard, or looking at things wrong. When she and Winnie had played the finding games, there were rules and clues. This time she seemed to be going it alone.

Each night the howling had become ear splitting, and

Nora was grateful her only neighbors were coyotes. While Liam, Robyn, and Byntwig were putting a brave face on, Nora knew that the Garnel was gaining power. She could feel it, and if she could, surely her mentors could. But she could see the wards in the garden wall were weakening. The evening meal was most often disrupted by the yowl and baying of the Garnel, and digesting became a challenge. Nora grew more determined to find a way with her limited skill to hoist the Garnel on his own petard. Yet she kept this determination to herself. It wasn't that she didn't want to share, it was that she felt she couldn't. So she searched the journals for some clue to the Achilles heel of the Garnel. Winnie had to know something. It had to be in the journals, it just had to be.

The hours with Byntwig and Robyn were spent in constant practice. Her incantations were juvenile, her kinetics lacked focus, and her potions…well, they were not working out. All this according to the elf, whose presence was surrounded by negative energies.

Liam tried to encourage her, but even he was failing in getting to her. She found them congregated having a hushed conversation; she knew it was about her. Nora sensed their disappointment, and had a feeling they were coming up with a contingency plan. Sneaking out for a breath of air, Nora made her way quietly down the moraine and stopped at the garden wall. This was her boundary line; this was her limit.

She felt the Garnel long before he made his appearance. He leaned on a tree and gave her a smarmy smile. Nora turned her back on him, but knew he was still there. She looked up the sculpted hillside to the garden and the house that Winnie had left her. The Garnel inched forward as far as the protective wards would allow him.

"Feeling inadequate?" he inquired.

Nora crossed her arms and chose not to acknowledge his query.

"Poor little mortal," he said in an unpleasant, surly tone. "Finding it all too hard? Why not just give in? This isn't really your battle, after all."

"This is your fault," she said in a huff.

Garnel was chuckling, then agreed. "Indeed."

Nora turned and looked at him. "And to you it's all just so funny and too amusing." Heat rose, from her heart to her head. She could feel it...hell, she could taste it! Standing so close to the wall, she could feel it vibrate.

His eyes slanted as he once more nodded. Nora could see he was most pleased with the way his little trick on Winnie had unfolded. He was doing nothing to hide his satisfaction.

She shook her head. "You're just despicable."

"Wait until you get to know me," he teased. "You'll really despise me before I'm done with you."

How in the world did Winnie get sucked in? she wondered to herself. *This guy is such a blowhard pig. Was she drunk?*

Nora put her own feelings and dislike of the Garnel aside for a moment. She gazed at him as if seeing him for the first time. Yes, in the physical form he was using, he was for the most part what some women would find appealing, and she was sure if he wanted to be he was capable of being charming. Not knowing how he'd tricked Winnie was a drawback, in her opinion. She wanted to shove his teeth, those gleaming white teeth that would turn to fangs, down his own throat so he'd choke on them, even though she knew that wasn't the most productive way to think. *He must think me a terrible fool, so why don't I just let him go on thinking that?* Slumping her shoulders, she lowered her eyes. "It's so unfair," she whimpered, praying he'd be the one to be sucked in. "This is just so hard because of you." The vibration in the wall increased.

The Garnel chuckled as he leaned back on the tree behind him. "Poor, weak little creature," he gloated. "You're hardly worth the effort."

Blood boiling, Nora controlled her desire to send him to the depths of the swamp, stuck up to his waist upside down, head first. She swallowed the bile and kept the poise of one who was broken and nearly submissive. "I just don't understand why you did this to me…." The words grated on her as she spoke them, but she prayed she'd get the answers that would give her clues to missing information.

"Don't flatter yourself," he sneered. "It's not you specifically; it's anyone who would have inherited the position of Guardian." He snorted rudely. "Not that you'd have been much of a challenge had I not trapped Winnie. You're not exactly adept, are you?" His disdain dripped. "You couldn't even find your way out of a wet paper bag."

He sounds like Connie! "Well, what did you expect?" She made herself sob. "I had no idea. And now…the world will…." She pretended to cry, poking herself in the eye to draw tears, and thinking the saddest thoughts she could in an effort to throw him off and keep him bragging.

The Garnel ate up her sorrow, and fed heavily on her distress. "Shall I keep you alive long enough to watch, I wonder?" he tormented. "Yes, perhaps that will be amusing."

He's so positive he's going to win, Nora worried. *There must be more to this than Robyn or Byntwig have told me…there must be.* She looked up, tears streaming down her face. "I mean nothing to you at all, do I?"

"Just an obstacle that must be cleared from my path," he said coldly. "A pitiful obstruction at best." He gave her a haughty stare. "It would have been so much more interesting if the other had been chosen. She would have given me a battle worth my time…and perhaps she'd have been more open to suggestions of a physical nature than even Winnie was."

"You were aware of us, even in your slumber?" she asked innocently, eyes widening.

"Aware," he mused, "does not begin to tell all that I experienced." He pushed off the tree and stood only feet from her, unable to cross the ward that Winnie had placed in the wall. But it was growing weaker as the time of Samhain drew near. "I fed off the other's lovely fortification of hatred for you. She was open to gentle directions, taking them much further than I could have hoped. And her brother," he smacked his lips. "What a tasty morsel of abhorrence and decadence he is."

Nora didn't like hearing this, but was glad the creature was in a boastful mood. *Keep talking,* she willed. *Tell me your secrets.*

"Between the two of them it was easy to keep you downtrodden and in the dust," he boasted.

"You did that to me?"

"As I would to anyone who was to be the heir!" he glowered. "Anyone who stands in the way of my freedom."

Balling her hands into fists, Nora forced herself to remain in a submissive mode. She drove her knee into the garden wall, drawing energy off it. The Garnel didn't seem to feel her true feelings, only the ones she was projecting. She prayed that she could continue to entice him to tell her what she wanted and needed to know. "You made Connie do all those things to me? You made her hate the Hollow and want to destroy it?"

"Guilty," he cackled.

"But…this place…is…special," she whimpered.

His black eyes hardened and he snarled darkly, "This place is a prison! Nothing more, nothing less." He moved closer and was repelled by the wards. "I've spent two hundred years trapped here, and for that your kind and all mankind will pay."

She wanted to poke him in the eye, or to slap him upside the head, but she chose to pull back and cower. "But all the innocent people…."

"Who cares about them?" the Garnel shouted. "For that matter, who cares about you?" He leaned forward, closer, to feed off her misery; the words wounded, as they were meant to. Nora allowed the hurt, for the greater good. "Do you think anyone would mourn your passing, even as noble as you may try to make it sound? Do you think…?" He closed his eyes for a moment to draw forth a name. "Daniel," he opened his eyes, "Would give two thoughts about you?"

Think about Daniel, she told herself. *Remember how much you cared about him at first. Feel the hurt…give this monster what he wants.* The painful memories flooded forward and overwhelmed her for a moment. "I thought he loved me."

The Garnel drank up the sorrow, the anguish and the suffering, like a cat lapping milk, growing almost drunk on the heady emotions. His eyes grew glassy. "He never did," he assured the girl. "It was easy to suggest to such a selfish man that he'd be better served to have an affair with that self-absorbed egotistical cousin of yours. Even without him ever having been here. Just his being in close proximity to her made him vulnerable to me. And she was only too willing to enjoy what he had to offer, like the greedy sexual predator that she is."

Nora winced. It was painful, but she pushed for more. "You did that?"

"Leaving you disconnected from the most primal of urges," he laughed coarsely. "Never to enjoy the simplest pleasures of human union." Disdainfully he added, "Virginal."

Why would he want a weakened Guardian to remain a virgin? she wondered. "That's cruel," she whispered. 'What power is there in a Guardian who isn't a virgin?'

The Garnel gazed at her with something she hadn't expected...longing. "I suffered, and so must you."

There was more to this, but what? "You left someone behind?" she asked with sympathy.

"No," he denied. But something in him told her that was false.

"I'm sorry," she said contritely, feeling sick as she did. In truth, she didn't feel sorry. She was glad he'd suffer for two hundred years. If she had any say there'd been two hundred more to follow. And another two hundred after that!

Still drinking in the wave of deep emotions, he crooned, "I shall keep you alive, long enough to purge my desires and longings...long enough to teach you what you've missed."

A lump gathered in Nora's throat. This fear, this sensation of panic, was real. He meant to use her virginal body; there was no mistaking his meaning. Looking up, she saw an ugly passion burning in his eyes. "Oh my God, no," she gasped before she turned to run quickly back up the hillside. The sun would be gone soon, and the wall would not protect her.

The Garnel, intoxicated under the influence of the raw emotions and fears, collapsed on the ground beyond the wall and laughed, unaware he'd given much too much information to Nora.

Nora took refuge in the house, having gone up to her bedroom and hiding away in the secret sanctuary. Cowering in a corner, balled up and rocking, she fretted over a fate that seemed unlikely to be prevented. Her breathing was labored, her heart raced not with joy but with horror. The roar of blood rushing in her ears was deafening. Panicked beyond what she had ever known, she curled up tighter. "Help me, someone, help me," she begged. "Aunts...all of you...help me!"

Above, the chandelier began to tinkle as crystal prisms struck one another. Soon the entire metal structure and the fine glass began to vibrate violently in answer to the girl's panic. Nora looked up, distracted from her own distress, fascinated by the sound and sight. Her body relaxed and the vibration came to an end. She leaned on the trunk she was seated next to.

"I wish I had an answer to this...if not from Winnie, from any other of my ancestors who were Guardians," she said aloud in supplication. "A little help would be deeply appreciated, ladies." Nora thought about all she'd learned in her weeks in training. Instinct kicked in. "I call upon the Belfry line," she said loudly. "Beyond space, beyond time. Gather here, in this secret place, and give this child all your grace." She wasn't sure where the words had come from, but the moment she'd spoken the words, she knew they were right. The room filled with the scents of lovely old and delicate perfumes. The chandelier tinkled softly, playfully, joyfully. Energy filled the room, and gave her encouragement.

A jolt shot through her as the trunk nudged her with a hard shove. Nora's head turned and she glared at the trunk. It was the oddly shaped Camelback trunk, and it shoved up against her again. She thought she had perhaps imagined it, but then the trunk bounced against her again, this time harder than the times before. Turning until she was on her hands and knees, Nora watched in fascination as the trunk seemed to be hopping in place. Then it began to shudder and vibrate, and as it did Nora noticed that the edge she'd been seated against seemed to not be fitted tightly against the other side edge. She looked more carefully and traced the seam with her fingers, looking for some like of latch system. When her fingers found it the entire end of the trunk fell open, revealing a hidden compartment. Notes on parchment, pages of drawings, and a book bound in heavy leather fell out. They spread on the floor, as in a set pattern.

Nora lifted one page and began to read the notes; her jaw dropped open. She studied the drawings and sifted through the pages of odds and ends. Finally, she opened the book with a soft gasp. She read the first page over and over, still leaning on the trunk. "Why, Aunt Harriet," she murmured. "You sly old witch."

Picking up the volumes of parchment pages and the elaborate drawings, she placed them spread out on the little tea table. Moving aside the tea set, she made room for all the pages and the leather bound book. Sitting down, she heard the tinkling of crystal above her. "Thank you, Aunt Harriet, you've saved my bacon," she said aloud. "I'll take it from here, darling."

~*~

Byntwig felt the change in the vibration of the house and noted the other two males didn't, but then neither of them was a fully-fledged mage. While both the elf and the Celt used magic, they didn't live and breathe it. The sharp, crisp sound of crystal sang out to him, and he smiled. With two days left before the showdown of Guardian and Garnel, he took a deep breath and put the outcome into the willing hands of Fate.

Robyn was fretting as he went over the latest notes that Nora had taken. "She's not getting it!"

Liam didn't want to agree, but he couldn't deny that Nora was nowhere near ready. "She's trying," he said defensively.

The elf glared at the dark Celt. "You've always had a soft spot for her…I think it's addled your brains."

"I'm not soft on the girl," Liam denied. His face was hard. "Besides, it wouldn't do for me to be…so."

"You've someone waiting?" Byntwig asked.

"My people chose my bride when I was young, and she was an infant. When the world is safe once more and the new Guardian is actively in place…I go home to wed," Liam said, as if it were common knowledge.

Robyn narrowed his gaze. "Then why have you been making moon eyes at the girl?"

"I haven't."

"You have so."

"You're reading things into my concern that are not

there," Liam denied. "She is part of my family...extended, to be sure, but no less a Belfry than I am. We share the same blood, and that is all."

Byntwig allowed the argument to continue, fascinated by the fact that Robyn wasn't defending Nora. He watched as the outraged elf seemed angrier at Nora than at Liam. "You don't like our little apprentice," the old troll accused the elf. "I wonder why that is?"

Robyn turned with a wounded expression on his face. "How can you say that? Have I not worked as hard as anyone to help her reach her goals?"

"You are harder on her than either of us," the old troll observed. "You also seemed the quickest to pronounce her incapable of completing her task."

"I realize it's through no fault of her own," Robyn said, sounding extremely haughty. "After all, she didn't have the benefit of being raised to use the powers that should be hers by birthright."

"Should be?" questioned the troll. "Do you doubt them?"

"Don't you?" Robyn began to pace, his elegant hands clasped behind his back. "She can't even speak Gaelic or basic Latin." His tone soured. "She has no idea of the wheel of the year, and she slacks off."

"Is that what you think?" Byntwig frowned. "You didn't volunteer for this assignment, did you?"

Cynical and suspicious of the old troll, the elf crossed his arms. "I don't see why that would be of importance."

Liam turned to Byntwig. "Is it important?"

"It may well be," the old mage advised. "Goodwyn, I am not casting a slur upon you," he soothed. "I'm saying you didn't want to be here in the first place."

Robyn frowned. "It was and is my duty, because I guided Winnie."

"But you're not happy about it," the troll finished.

"No," Robyn admitted freely. "Why should I be happy? This latest addition of the Belfry Guardian is not up to the caliber of others of her lineage."

"Don't be in such haste to judge her," warned the troll. "What we have here, gentlemen, is a diamond in the rough."

"Nonsense," Robyn protested. "She can't levitate a paper, she can't recite the simplest of spells, and she's got no sense of timing! The creature cannot even make a simple potion." He paced anew. "She's hopeless, and we are doomed."

Liam frowned. "Think of how difficult this is for her," he suggested softly. "She never had any idea of who and what she was. If you are going to find fault, look at Winnie."

"Oh, I have plenty of faults to heap upon her as well," Robyn stated hotly. "She should have known better than to be taken in by the Garnel. She knew full and well what was expected of a Guardian…she'd been trained before she took up the title." His eyes were full of disdain. "I don't see why fate would entrust the safety of the world to the women of this line."

"Fate chooses who fate requires," the troll said sagely. "Not all the Guardians of this world are men."

"Women of every walk of life are softer than men, and everyone knows that mortal women are much weaker willed than their male counterparts," Robyn stated.

Liam thought back to the fire he'd witnessed in Nora's eyes. "I have my doubts to the veracity of that statement. No, my fine elf friend, I don't think that mortal women are weaker than men. I think they know a strength we are too proud to admit to, and are unable to understand."

"And would your beloved understand this praise you heap upon this other woman?" Robyn asked, content that she would not. "This woman you say you don't love."

"Megan would understand," Liam assured the elf. "She's a superior woman." He added softly, "Much like Nora Belfry."

Byntwig heard the tinkle of crystal again. "She's unique," he uttered with a wicked smile.

Robyn snarled as he took a seat. "She's a disaster, and we are doomed!"

~*~

Nora was fascinated by Harriet's detailed drawings, not only of the Garnel, but those of the Hollow. Each was a work of art, done with a loving hand. "What a wise old crone you must have been," she murmured. "How I wish I had known you in person, not just from these pages." The air filled with soft perfume and a warm loving sense of purpose. Nora basked in it as if it were a hug, for in truth it was as comforting as an embrace from a kindly elder. "I'm learning so much from you," Nora said aloud. "Thank you for coming to my rescue."

The trunk thumped and Nora laughed. "You too, trunk."

Each time she placed a drawing aside to read the corresponding note, the crystal in the chandelier reacted. The sound was reassuring and soothing, as it gave encouragement to the girl who was gleaning years of knowledge, not just absorbing but understanding. "You had a better eye than even Winnie," Nora commented to the spirit she felt near.

She was aware that Harriet wouldn't answer, as it would jeopardize the girl's mission. "You saw the moraine in a way she couldn't." Turning over the notes and the drawings, she took a deep breath. "If only Winnie had listened to you, Aunt Harriet."

The trunk thumped once more, and a tiny little locket fell out of the hidden compartment. Picking it up, Nora recognized the motif at once...the Belfry coat of arms. But there was a difference to this one. The background was not the usual shield...it was the moraine and the garden wall. Opening the little ornament, she found strands of hair, four in all. "The chain of lineage," she whispered. "First Guardian of the Hollow, to the last." Reaching up, she pulled a single strand of her own hair and joined it with the rest. "And the present," she said, firmly closing the locket before placing the chain about her own neck. "We are together." Energy raced through every fiber of her being. The crystal shook, making a lovely musical sound, its light bathing her in a shower of luminescence.

Chapter 16

Nora came down to dinner inwardly more calm, not that Robyn or Liam noticed. Byntwig watched her with his amber eyes, but didn't say anything to give his thoughts away, and for this she was grateful. The meal passed in a dark cloud of silence, and the mood was somber as two of the mentors feared what was coming. Falling back into the patterns that had been hers for life, she found it easier to observe her companions. Robyn didn't notice the reverting, and Liam seemed lost in his own thoughts. Only Byntwig seemed to be aware of what she was doing. His silence sealed his willingness to be party to her subterfuge.

Excusing herself from the table, Nora went up the stairs to her room. She closed the door, as was her custom, and then moved swiftly to the hidden passage in the closet and up to the sanctuary. She inspected Aunt Harriet's trunk again and found a secret compartment on the other side of the trunk, just opposite the side that had held the drawings and parchment notes and the pendant she now wore. In this compartment she found more parchments, and also a book full of drawings, notes, and bits of plants.

Gathering all the items and spreading them out on the tea table, Nora went back and opened the lid of the trunk to remove the compartment that held the family pictures and mementos that Harriet had treasured. She was glad that each photo and tintype had marks on them identifying the persons in each shot. More and more of them were shots of the members of the family who had lived here. They were all shots taken in summer by the looks of the garments they wore. But not all the shots were taken in the garden; some were taken in the meadow. Nora recognized the area; it was part of what Winnie had called the nature walk. It was where she had tested the girls and David on their knowledge of the flora and fauna.

Taking a piece of chalk that had been tucked into one of the compartments, Nora moved to the wall that was a mural of the moraine. She marked off the footings of the house, then the path down to the garden wall where she'd seen the Garnel. She marked the meadow and the swamp. Standing back, she let her eyes gather in the information that had always been before her very eyes. Winnie might not have been able to teach her, but it didn't stop her from giving the girl clues in her teachings of the Hollow. She looked at the little book with the bits and pieces of plants. She marked on the mural where each had come from, again standing back to study the progress.

Tapping her chin with her fingers, she decided to add the names on the photos to the mural. The oldest of the photos were of Agatha, and they dated to about the Civil War. One of the photos even had the name of Brady on its cover. She remembered her grandfather John talking about the family having been clients of Brady during those days. The forge started by Agatha's father had made the family powerful, and had given them position and wealth. It wasn't uncommon back then for such people to have Brady come to work his magic in capturing their images. Nora wondered if the early camera had captured anything else. She sat down with the early photos and began to inspect them more closely.

It was hardly noticeable at first, but on closer inspection there was something in the image that shouldn't be there. It was more than a shadow, for it had definite shape and volume. There behind Aunt Agatha, standing beside the mantel of the family home, was something that shouldn't have been there...a creature with eyes that looked surprised by the photo-flash bar. She had missed it the first time she'd studied the photo, but now she was seeing with new eyes. "Well, I'll be," she said with a smile. "An imp."

She put the early photo aside, and searched the pile for the one of Agatha at Misty Hollow. Nora had heard the story of how Agatha had inherited a great fortune, and had turned down many a suitor. She had been told that the woman was independent, and had spoken for women's rights back at the time of the Civil War. She had taken charge of her finances against her father's objections. The fact that she'd done exceedingly well had caused quite a ruckus in the family. It was Agatha who had purchased the land that would be handed down from one Guardian to another.

Nora went back to the diary that Agatha had left, and the

one left by Harriet. Each read like concise history archives. Agatha's began just prior to her having the bought the Hollow, and spoke of the moraine in reverent terms. Nora realized the woman was an early version of what were being called ecologists and conservationists today. It was carefully written, with no mention of the Garnel or of the position of Guardian. Going back to the tintype that was dated, Nora verified that it was before Agatha inherited her fortune and built the house. Yet there was the imp; in Belfry house there was an imp.

"Aggie," she said with a gasp of realization. "You had a familiar long before you became the Guardian! So you were already practicing...." The chandelier above her tinkled in answer, and Nora felt a tingling like fingers touching her arm. "When this is over," she whispered, "We will need to talk…there is so much I need to know." Liam had said there were Belfry witches and wizards long before a Belfry became a Guardian, and now Nora had proof.

She went to the picture of Harriet sitting on the steps of the foundation of the cottage at the turn of the century. Beside her in the shadows was not an imp, but another creature that shouldn't have been there. Nora smiled; it was strangely comforting seeing the little familiar so close to Harriet. Then came the shots of Winnie and Harriet over the years, seated together, with the creatures in the shadows as the house had been built, and then as the additions went on. So many creatures that Nora was taken aback. She had a hunch that not all were familiars…some just liked to congregate at the Hollow. Nora had said to Connie that the Hollow was special. She'd meant it, but now she realized it was special to more than just the Guardians. The Hollow was part of the old magic.

Reading Harriet's words, Nora saw how different, in many ways, she had been from Agatha, and yet so alike. There was a common theme through both diaries. She longed to read the words of other women who had lived in this family. She could feel the strength of each of the women whose strands of hair were encased in the locket begin to surge in her own veins. She had always felt close to Winnie; now she was beginning to feel close to the ones who'd come before her. The ones who had formed Winnie's path. No, the ones who had formed the path of the Belfry Guardian, starting with Agatha, who had purchased the land. Then to Anna, who, according to Harriet's diary, had set up the wall that kept the Garnel in the swamplands, and who had died young of a fever. Harriet, the one who built the house. Winnie, who, until she got cocky, had held the line. Now Nora joined the line, her hair twined in the pendant with the others.

The howl outside deep in the wooded area broke her reverie. There were only two days left, and in that forty-eight hours she would have to convince the men who had been sent to help her that she had given up. For her plan to work she had to make them feel they were the only ones left to protect the world.

Robyn would be easily convinced...he had the least faith in her. Liam would be more difficult, and she needed him to be completely taken by surprise. The last thing she needed was his interference. If he had the slightest idea of what she was up to he'd try to stop her; or worse, he'd try to rescue her. She couldn't afford to be stopped, and she sure as hell didn't need to be rescued. Byntwig was the only member of her companions she had no qualms about. He was a mage; he would let her do what she had to do, no questions asked and no worthless recriminations. Nora knew what he'd say; "A mage has to do what a mage has to do." They were of the same cloth, she and the troll, and he would not be a problem. If anything, he was her most important ally.

She closed up the diary, placed it over the parchments, and moved to the door. Giving the room one last glance, she switched off the lights. The passageway was narrow; nevertheless, it felt safe and secure. Once in her room, she listened; the second floor was very quiet. She cracked open her door and listened until she heard the faint sounds of conversation down in the parlor. They had not missed her; they had been down there the entire time and not missed her, foolish men. The clock on her night table told her she had spent a good three hours up in the sanctuary. It was a relief not to have to worry about questions she had no answers to. Or to have to pretend that she didn't feel the magic that now surged through her. It was as if she'd always known magic, always felt its electric vibes racing through her. Perhaps she had, and not known what it was, or why she'd always felt she was different from the rest of the family. Different from Connie. If what Byntwig had said was true, then she'd been born with the gift of magic. It had been there, dormant, until she was ready to accept it, and use it as the new Guardian. Perhaps hitting rock bottom in being trained by these outsiders, and turning to the sanctuary had all been part of some master plan.

What was hidden up in the sanctuary was for her use and her knowledge alone. If her plan worked she would tell them what she could. Some things would have to remain secret, as they had for other Belfry Guardians. Things that could and would only be shared with *her* heir would remain private. A smile crept to Nora's lips; she was thinking of the future, a future Belfry Guardian. This was better progress than making an envelope move, or understanding Celtic Gaelic. There would be a future for a new Belfry Guardian to live in, she was sure.

Nora changed for bed, switched off her lamp, and pulled the covers tight about her like a cocoon to protect her from the things that could not be seen in the night. Thinking about the strange little creatures in the photos, she pondered if she'd been granted a familiar, what would it look like? She looked at the shadows that were dancing in the dimness of her room, and wondered if one or more were creatures that the human eye chose not to see. Would she see them if she truly wanted to?

Impulsively she sat up and whispered into the darkness, "All you shadowed creatures that herein dwell, gather round and bid me well."

While she still couldn't exactly see them clearly, she could feel the closeness of the things that most humans chose not to see. It was reassuring and encouraging, and she had a feeling that her words had a better flow than before. She knew that it had felt right when she'd said them. Here in the dark room, she knew she was safe and guarded by the creatures in the dark. Laying back into her pillow, she closed her eyes and smiled. She was the Guardian.

Nora knew that what she had planned for the next day was going to be difficult. Tricking Robyn and Liam didn't sit well with her, and she was relieved she didn't have to resort to such deceit with Byntwig as well. Something deep within her soul told her that the old troll would go along with whatever she planned. She was a mage in the making, a user of magic, and a believer. Byntwig was on her side.

~*~

Byntwig felt the changes in the vibrations of the house, knowing he was more in tune because of his being a mage. The sounds of crystal tinkling when the girl had left them clued him in, and he was somewhat mystified that the elf and Liam were oblivious to the sounds coming from the upper floor. The house, because it was a house built to absorb the energies of the moraine, seemed to have a constant hum. Again the old troll wondered at the lack of reaction from his companions. The changes were subtle, to be sure, but they were there. He listened to the elf going on about how they had failed. Much as he would have liked to object, he felt drawn to keep his own silence on the subject. The little Belfry witch was coming along, and he wasn't about to give her away, not when so much depended on her.

~*~

"*If* she fails," Liam protested. "You seem to deem that it's a given that she will fail." He directed his words to the elf.

Robyn's face was a stony mask. "Can you honestly see her succeeding?"

Liam wanted to say he could, but it would have been a lie. "It is unfortunate that she was deprived of proper training for so long."

"Unfortunate?" spat the elf. "It was catastrophic!"

Liam couldn't argue that point. "No fault of her own,"

he reminded the other. "What happened was long before she was ever born!"

Robyn glared at him. "Fault or not, we have a disaster on our hands. She is not ready to face the Garnel. He'll walk over her like a welcome mat, and sweep the world with his evil."

Byntwig murmured, "You care so much for this world?"

"No," Robyn admitted. "My fears are not for this realm. I worry more about what it will mean to the lands beyond the mists. To the fairylands and the refuges we've forged. The Garnel will not overlook that we backed the Guardians!" His blue eyes darkened. "If the mortal Guardian cannot keep that thing harnessed, we are all doomed. The Garnel will neither ignore nor forget what we did."

"But you don't care one way or the other what happens to the mortals, do you?"

Calmly Robyn addressed the troll. "Do you, Troll?"

"Actually, I do," Byntwig announced, pulling his beard thoughtfully. "I have a fondness for them, these fragile creatures. They have hidden strengths and talents, and I do care for them. But my kind and theirs have a rather tangled web of history."

"And mine doesn't?" Robyn challenged.

Giving the elf a trollish grin, the old man shrugged. "One would think you'd be more defensive given your kind's history with the mortal realm. Everyone thinks that elves are wonderful and full of goodness and light." He chuckled harshly. "Are you the exception to that rule?"

Insulted to his core, Robyn's mouth dropped open. "How dare you?"

"How dare you?" Byntwig replied coldly. "You stand

here condemning that girl before she's even taken one step."

"I'm stating facts," protested the affronted elf. "She's not going to be able to do the task that is required of her. She's a weak link, a broken wall…she's an imposter!"

"An imposter?" countered Liam. "She's the heir to the title Belfry Guardian; there's no mistaking that."

"She's not good enough," Robyn argued. "Fate has dealt us a blow, and we are all doomed."

Byntwig turned to Liam. "What say you?"

"I have my fears for the girl," he admitted. "I know Nora has fire, but will it be enough? I don't know." He sighed deeply before he added, "I too worry about the lands beyond the mists, but also for the ones I've left behind beyond the sea."

"You fear you'll not see them again?" Byntwig asked.

"I fear I will, and will not be able to prevent the devastation that Garnel means to inflict on one and all."

The old troll stood up and looked at his companions before pronouncing in judgment, "What will be, will be; it is what it is." He yawned. "I'm off to my bed, I suggest you gentlemen be off to yours."

Chapter 17

Before the dawn the shadow creatures awakened Nora and pulled her toward the hidden passage. She understood there was something they wanted her to see, needed her to see. When her fingers reached for the light switch, an obstacle prevented her from touching it. Taking it as a sign, she allowed the energies to take the lead and place her where they wanted her, where they needed her to be. She was facing the beautiful circular window that graced the pitch of the roof, and the wall with its intricate pattern of leading. Nora wondered what it was that could be so important that the shadow creatures needed to show her. She was under the impression she knew the view of that window already. Still the urgings she was receiving were trying to keep her focused on the glass. She slowed her breathing, focused, and watched. Moments later Nora saw for the first time the hidden etchings on the glass, etchings so fine that one would miss them unless the light hit them just right.

She rushed forward, studying the lines and the markings. "Well, I'll be," she muttered. "It's a Guardian road map!"

~*~

When she came down to breakfast, she wore a subdued expression on her face and slumped her shoulders. Robyn glared at her, and Liam said little. Now and again she and the old troll exchanged a glance or two. His face was passive, and didn't give his thoughts away. When the meal ended she obediently followed the old troll out of the kitchen and into the nook, where she was supposed to be working on incantations.

"I understand what you are doing." Byntwig rolled out a scroll for her to inspect, and bending close to the seated young mortal woman, he whispered in her ear. "Tis a dangerous game you play; however, I shall follow your lead, *Guardian*."

She didn't react; she kept her features passive but gave him a nod.

"You have but to show the way," he added before he moved away.

"I don't understand this passage," she said, loud enough to be heard by any who wished to listen in, pointing to something on the scroll.

"We've gone over that before," he said patiently.

"I need to go over it again," she insisted. Both troll and mortal heard the fussing coming from the kitchen. Green eyes met amber, and the pact was sealed. "I keep missing things," she said, knowing the troll would understand.

"Then look closer," he advised.

She gave him a curt smile. "I'm trying to." Her voice tightened, but her eyes were looking past the troll to where the elf was lurking, trying to hear what was being said, what he had no part in. He had been so hard on her, and now Nora wondered if he were perhaps a weak link, easily swayed by the creature she would do battle with.

Byntwig became aware of the other lurking, and said, "Nora, we have gone over this time and time again." He hoped she'd pick up on the cue. "Surely you know what it is."

Nora caught the cue; she slumped her shoulders even more and lowered her eyelids, giving anyone looking in on the scene an impression of dejection. "This is so hard," she whimpered. It irked her that she had to use this ruse, and she was glad that the troll was party to the charade. With his support and his guidance, she'd made strides. Now she had to use all she'd learned.

Noise from the hall betrayed the elf, and he moved away. Byntwig whispered, "You don't trust him?"

Nora shook her head. "It's not that," she mouthed. "I need him to feel I'm hopelessly behind. The Garnel feeds on that kind of negative energy. The more hopeless Robyn thinks I am, the better. I think Garnel has been twisting the elf, playing on his disdain for humanity. Well, two can play that game."

A gnarled hand pulled at the snowy white beard on his chin. "You're using him to give the Garnel the wrong signals?"

"He's an effective decoy, and so willing to see me as not up to his standards," Nora whispered. "I shouldn't have accused him of being a refugee from a Ren Fair."

Byntwig looked at her questioningly for a moment, considering the implications and repercussions that would follow. "It could work. Robyn comes from very vain stock."

"It has to work," she confirmed. "So do me a favor, scold me."

For a moment he stared at her. "Nora," he said, louder and sharply, putting the hushed tones aside. "You're not trying hard enough." He winked at her and went stoic. Anyone who was observing them would only see what the old troll wanted them to see. He used his knowledge of expectations, and gave a grand performance. If it hadn't been so serious, Nora would have kissed him.

~*~

Garnel was growing stronger, and the negative vibes coming from the cottage were restoring his energy levels to nearly full power. Someone in the cottage wasn't happy, someone wasn't feeling entirely sure, and one person was feeling utterly doomed…surely that one must be the unlucky girl. It was a complicated feast of delights, and it gladdened him that the esoteric foundation that the household had been built upon seemed to be crumbling from within. This little mortal would be no match for him, and soon he'd have his freedom.

The wards that had been placed as protections were growing weaker and weaker; soon they would fade altogether. Winnie had only fortified what others had begun, but in the last years her strengths had dwindled. Garnel had not expected the heir to be so attached to the Hollow. He had done a great deal during the girl's childhood to stymie her; her cousins had been a great help in that. They were not really as strong as they believed they were, but they were a fine pair of protagonists against the other.

He wondered why it was she had not fallen to pieces

under their barrage years ago. He had given both David and Connie encouragement; he had watched as they tore down the confidence of the younger girl. Yet she had remained steadfastly devoted to Winnie. Garnel had grudgingly admired the devotion even while he tried to break the girl. His efforts had not been in vain, he told himself. She was little more than a mouse, afraid of her own shadow. He had made sure that no one could see the real worth of her being. Even her sham of an engagement had been his doing. Just as he had tricked Winnie, he had set out traps for Nora. While other young women were blooming, she had seemingly gone dormant. She had never blossomed into the beauty that her youth had promised, nor had she ever tasted love. She was alone in this world, an outsider even within her own family ranks. And it was all his doing.

    He had expected her to crumble, to tremble and to wither under Connie's authority. She by all rights should have signed away the rights to the cottage, and it would have insured his freedom. Without a Guardian on the watch, he would have been free to walk across the useless wards come All Hollow's Eve. He had calculated all it would take, and the girl should have bent to the stronger will of Connie. But Nora had resisted.

    Still, he took comfort in the fact that because he'd prevented her from being properly apprenticed, she was virtually useless as a Guardian. She had no training, no skill, no guidance, and he would walk over her, grinding her into the dust beneath him. A sneer came to his lips as he gorged himself on the feelings of desolation and failure coming from the cottage. He had utterly destroyed the girl without any resistance. Finishing her off would be a sweet finale to his years of imprisonment. Poor, pitiful, creature that she was, having been deprived of all that should have by rights been hers as the heir. He would keep his ugly, threatening promise; keep her alive long enough to see her world enslaved and destroyed under his wrath. The thought of keeping her as a pathetic and paltry pet pleased him. He would corrupt her; she would be even more base than her cousin Connie when he was through.

It was laughable to compare the dark eyed, dark haired vixen to the mouse. Corrupting the vixen had been almost too easy, as she had sinister and malicious depths naturally. She had willingly taken his directions from the start. Her brother was even more easily swayed, but he was weak and easily pushed about. He was a coward as well, and needed the protections of his older sister from being discovered as weak in the world. Garnel had tired of the boy quickly, lost interest in what use he could have been. He had placed all his concentration on the vixen, and she had not disappointed him, right down to her betrayal of Nora with the man that he'd arranged to be interested in the mouse. It was a delightful devastation, and it had caused the mouse to draw even deeper into herself. It should have been the death blow, but somehow she'd survived. Her self-worth was shattered, confidence destroyed, and her heart an empty shell, and yet she still survived.

Garnel turned to look toward the cottage in the distance, and he pondered. She should have crumbled; she should have withered and turned to dust. Yet she had not. She had not even made public the betrayal; she had quietly accepted the termination of her engagement and drawn deeper into her own quiet world. She had quiet strength, and if she were not the Guardian heir he might have admired her for that quiet reserve of strength. He resented the hell out of it, but he also had to credit the girl. She was far more decent to Connie than Connie had been to her.

He wondered what she might have been had he not interfered in her life. Would she have blossomed into a beauty? Would she have grown into that natural grace that the Belfry women seemed to own in abundance? Would she have known love? It was odd that he found himself feeling resentful and jealous of any man who would have awakened her. She was only a mortal, and a mousy one at that, and he chided himself for the weakness of pitying her. The feeling didn't leave; it lingered and gnawed at him. He remembered her when she was prepubescent, just before her body took its first steps into young womanhood. She had never been the radiant beauty that Connie was. She had not the vigor or the vivaciousness, but she had dignity, and quiet grace.

Nora had been smaller, more slender than Connie, and while the vixen took that as a sign of weakness, it had in truth been something far more. Nora, in her own tranquility, seemed to feed gently off the serene surroundings. She was in tune with nature, and could live in harmony with the creatures that cohabited in the Hollow. She didn't need fancy garments or gaudy jewels, she needed only the simplest of things. Just as Winnie had once been, before he tricked her into dancing Skyclad with him.

Garnel shook himself. Where were these thoughts coming from? Surely he didn't have sympathy for the one who had been chosen to be his keeper? That would be like pouring salt into his years of wounds. She was nothing, just a mortal, he told himself harshly. She was to be walked on, crushed, and destroyed.

Movement in the garden of the cottage drew his attention. He watched from afar as the dejected girl took refuge in the now empty garden space. All the harvest had been collected, and what was left looked like a desolate and barren plot of ground. Autumn was nearly over...winter would be here soon, and the greenery was gone. His dark eyes watched as she moved at a snail's pace amongst the remains of stalks and ornamental grasses. Her face was pained, and that should have given him satisfaction. He found it disturbing that it did not. She looked pale, and dark circles were noticeable under her enchanting green eyes.

Garnel turned away *Enchanting*? he pondered. Had he really found her eyes to be so? He looked back, and watched her trying to come to terms with her failure. *I wonder what it would have been like had I not been driven to destroy you.* Garnel observed that she was alone. He could feel the negative energies from the cottage, and understood that her mentors had given up all hope. He had won; there was only her surrender to be made, and he should have been elated. It disturbed him that instead of wishing to celebrate, he felt cheated.

She was coming down the hill, as she often did when things in the cottage became too much a burden for her to bear. While not a beauty, even in her humble attire and unadorned state the girl had *presence*, more so now in her defeat than Connie had ever had in victory. Garnel moved closer, drawn like a moth to a flame. He waited until she settled on the wall before he made his presence known.

"Problems, Heir?" he taunted, but in a softer tone than he'd intended. He could accept she was an heir to the title, but he wasn't about to grant that she was in any way shape or form the Guardian.

"Go away," she murmured pathetically. She covered her face with her hands as she rested her chin on her raised knees.

He couldn't pass the wall; Winnie's wards were still enforced, weaker than before but still preventing him from entering the grounds proper of the garden and the cottage. Hallowed ground, and he dared not try to enter. "Harder than you thought it would be?" he inquired.

"Yes," she moaned.

Garnel wished there were no bindings, no bounds that he couldn't pass. He had a desire to comfort the little heir, and that unhinged and troubled him. "I promise you," he said, trying to sound less threatening. "I will end it all quickly for you. I owe you that much." It was a lie, but it was such a little thing that he didn't really think it mattered. There was no way he was going to let her end be quick or painless.

She looked up, eyes brimming with fresh tears. "And you think I should be grateful for such consideration? I'm supposed to protect the entire world from you, and you think I should be appreciative and indebted that you're promising to end my life quickly?" She shook with anger and frustration. "I realize I mean nothing to you…to anyone…but give me the benefit of having some importance. Don't patronize me!"

Garnel hunkered down, cutting the distance in their gazes. "Nora Belfry," he said firmly. "Do you think I'd have gone to the difficulty of dealing you such a fate if it were not for the fact that I know you'd have been a force to deal with?" It was out, and he was perplexed as to why he'd said it.

"You cheated," she accused.

He nodded slowly. "I did."

"And you're going to stand there and tell me it's because you feared me?" She sounded exasperated and unbelieving.

"You would have been far too strong to battle," he acknowledged. It was as if he couldn't help himself, or stop the words from coming out. It was the truth, and it burned even as the words passed his lips. But he couldn't stop it.

"You couldn't have known that when you…tricked Winnie." She wiped the bitter tears away with her hand. "I don't even know how or why…but you couldn't have known."

Garnel paused. His desires to protect the mortal from more hurt countered his wishes to inflict that hurt, on her, on her line, on all humankind. "I assure you, I knew you to be a worthy opponent long before you were born," he glowered. "Even I can read the stars, Heir."

"So you made sure I'd be weakened," she accused.

"I want my freedom," he glowered. Their eyes locked, green ones full of sorrow and frustration, black ones full of fury. Garnel leaned as close as the wards would allow. "I will have my freedom. And you and your helpers will pay for having locked me here for two hundred years."

"Over my dead body," she whimpered, not sounding very convincing.

"If need be," he assured. His features softened, and his eyes burned with a darker desire than just freedom. "It does not have to be so," he suggested wickedly. "You don't have to die for this world…a world that does not even value you, Nora Belfry. You can save yourself."

"Save myself." She pulled back in horror. "What are you suggesting?"

"Surrender to me," he tempted enticingly. "Your body, your mind, your heart, and your soul," he murmured in a soft, low voice that beguiled with unspoken promises of forbidden pleasures. "I offer you what I have offered no other Guardian…I offer life. Give yourself freely to me, and I will spare you." He heard the offer, and at first thought he was just toying with her, as he had Winnie. But then something gave him pause. Perhaps it was that he'd been lonely, but something about the heir filled voids. Then he knew the dreadful truth of it…he wanted her.

"Give myself…to…you?"

His eyes lingered here and there as they journeyed over her seated on the wall. "There are a myriad of pleasures I could teach you," he said intriguingly. "I can take your soul to places that the man who was engaged to you never dreamed of. I can make your body sing songs you've imagined in your darkest thoughts." It was meant to be beguiling, but he couldn't keep the darkness from his inflection. He wanted her to join him in the darkness. "You don't have to die without experiencing the pleasures of the body."

Her eyes widened in alarm, but he noted that her heart was racing.

"Why not allow yourself what no one else would allow you? Live Nora, live to the fullest. Give yourself to me, and I will show you what no mortal ever could."

"You want me to forget that I'm all that stands between

you and—"

"You don't have to stand between," he tempted with passion. "It's not your battle, it never was."

"I may not have created this situation," she whispered tersely. "But I inherited it."

"In effect," he teased gently, "You inherited me. So why not enjoy your inheritance? Let me guide you in the ways of the pleasures of the flesh. I will allow you to live, and you will be at my side as I take back all that I was deprived of."

"What you are suggesting is monstrous," she whispered.

"Can you deny that you find me…intriguing?" Nora shook her head; he knew the answer before she admitted it. Her body was betraying her, just as Winnie's had betrayed her. The unknowing and deprived girl's resistance to him was waning. "I offer you not only life, Nora, but a life full of passion and pleasure. Give yourself to me. You won't be disappointed." Nora's lips parted; her eyes filled with unrequited desires and passions that were foreign to her. He was still leaning as close to the barrier as he could. "You have twenty-four hours in which to decide your fate," he forewarned gently. "I will await your answer."

"Where?" she asked in a soft voice.

"I have a lair," he told her in a sinister way. "Come to me there, either to surrender or to die." He motioned to the swamplands in the heart of the Hollow. "Tomorrow the mists will rise, the wards will fall, and I will either be free with you at my side, or beneath my feet. The choice is yours, Nora Belfry." His eyes danced with the desires of a darkness no mortal could grasp, but he could see this mortal was intrigued, if not completely captivated. "Come to me, Nora. Surrender to me and live." He stood up. "Or come to battle me and die."

"You give me little choice," she whimpered sadly.

"Your skills are no match to mine," he warned. "Come to me, accept the pleasures I offer…or die trying to save a world that does not care about you and the struggle between good and evil." Nora lowered her chin back to her knees. "You have twenty-four hours, use them well," he suggested before he turned and walked away from her. He could hear her sobs as he departed.

Chapter 18

Once she was certain the Garnel had truly departed her presence, she unfolded herself and got off the wall. Keeping her head down and allowing the tears and frustrations to continue to swathe her, she headed back to the house. Liam tried to reach out to her, and she sobbed loudly as she rushed past him, not allowing his fingers to touch her. The elf stood in the kitchen, giving her disparaging looks. The troll kept his distance, as if prearranged. Quickly Nora rushed up to her room, locked the door, and without delay moved up to the sanctuary of the hidden room. Only when she reached its safety did she halt the stream of tears, take a deep cleansing breath, and collapse to the floor. It had been the performance of a lifetime, and no one but the Garnel had witnessed it. She was grateful he didn't realize how much energy she'd drawn off the wall. She'd been careful not to draw so much that the wall might give her away. Even with the help of the wall she was feeling drained.

She lay within the intricate, complex design that she'd not really taken notice of until recently. "A circle of protection," she said knowingly as she lay there, regrouping. "You all could have warned me," she said aloud to her spiritual guides. "Ya could have tipped me off that he can be devastatingly persuasive." Her heart was still racing as she gave consideration to his offer. "Damn, but he can be one dead sexy beast when he wants to. No wonder Winnie screwed up!"

The chandelier above her tinkled as if in agreement.

Taking another cleansing breath, she exhaled until her lungs were clear. "Step one achieved. My mentors, or at least two out of three, are sure I'm unable to accomplish my role. Thank God and Goddess the troll was pretty hard to read; thank all that is holy, he is on my side," she said mostly to herself. "Step two, the beast is baited." She lay sprawled out in the circle, letting the magical energy refresh her. "Step three, I've received *'an offer I can't refuse,'*" her tone mocked. She closed her eyes and relaxed. "This was easier than I thought it would be. Good thing I've had lots of practice turning on the water works." The energy in the circle helped her compose herself. There was a sharp note from the chandelier above, and Nora nodded. "I know, I know, we're not at the finish line yet...," she admonished herself in a gentle tone. "Let's not get cocky; that's what got Winnie in trouble."

Again the crystals above her in the light fixture tinkled in agreement. Nora sighed, and allowed her body to absorb the restorative energies. Her alone time here in the attic with the journals of her ancestors had taught her a great deal. She hadn't thought that being so close to the Garnel would be nearly as draining, but it had been. It had been imperative that the creature believed her to be weak, but she was grateful for the grounding this circle of protection offered. "I should get an award for this performance," she muttered to herself once she felt more like herself.

Nora hadn't expected to be so taken with the Garnel; he'd never impressed her up until now. It had to be the weakening wards, which Nora had a myriad of questions about. Starting with how they had been created, and how they were maintained, let alone how they worked. But for now, their failing played into her plan. "You should have warned me, Aunt Harriet," she chided aloud. "I intend once this is over and done with to make sure the next generation knows and is prepared." Slowly she pulled herself up after turning over and using her upper arms to brace her weight. "Okay Harry, let's open that bag of tricks you put aside, and see what we have to work with." She crawled over to the trunk filled with the treasures of her ancestor. She still felt a bit drained, and was happy she didn't have to fend off Robyn and his negative energies. Fending off the Garnel's sexual energies and his suggestions had taken more energy than she was used to expending.

She sorted down through the layers of Harriet's belongings. At the very bottom of the trunk was a bundle that had been carefully wrapped and secured with twine. Beneath the bundle was a little box containing a pair of kidskin slippers and two vials; the vials were marked with rune symbols, and Nora set them aside. She marveled at the slippers; without trying them on Nora was certain that they would fit her like a glove. A fact that would have troubled her eight weeks ago, but today, she accepted as a foregone truth.

She placed the box and the bundle on the floor, turned, and sat with her back braced on the trunk. Taking a deep breath, she pulled the bundle into her lap. Her fingers made quick work of the twine, and the heavy tissue that acted like a wrapper opened to reveal the contents of the parcel. Folded neatly was a woven lightweight wool cloak in dove gray... it was plain, nothing spectacular or ostentatious. Even the clasp was plain, just a simple metal frog loop on either end with a hook and eye in the center. The quality of the wool was excellent, and it had weathered its stay in the trunk extremely well; in fact, it looked brand new. Nora wondered if it had ever been worn by Harriet, or if it were a secret weapon prepared for some future generation. From the way it was wrapped, she suspected the latter. It didn't feel like it held the vibe of any other Belfry witch.

Under the wool cloak was a gauzy garment that looked more like an expensive nightgown. The fabric showed no sign of wear, nor did it give away its age. It was a soft shade of mauve over a layer of gray. Both layers were thin as a whisper, moved with the ease of butterfly wings, and had pretty lace sashays between layers that smelled of lavender. "Good God and Goddess, Harry, do you expect me to seduce him?" she exclaimed as she inspected the garment. After she'd given it a thorough going over, she was certain it had never been worn. "Look, old girl, I don't mind being used as bait," she murmured. "But this is pushing it. What you're asking is... indecent."

She found a handwritten note under the filmy garment.

Dearest descendant. She recognized the handwriting as that of Harriet Belfry. It was a finer touch than that of Winnie Belfry, whose handwriting was a hurried scrawl in comparison. *If the shadows I've seen are any indication, there has been a terrible gap formed in our never ending chain. I blame myself for not warning Winnie to be more steadfast, as I see her to be our weakest link. She is a dear child, and I love her dearly, as if she were mine own, but she can be such a ninny. If the shadows that I foresee come to pass, Fate has chosen, in her wisdom, to give us the means to overcome the obstacle that is in your way.*

In this bundle you find sacred garments, which are to be used only in case of dire emergency. And if you're reading this, it's a dire emergency, make no mistake! The cloak has been woven with great care; it will cover not only your body, but your intents. Within its seams are amulets to protect and guide you, my dearest child. The gown is designed to entice and lure the Garnel into being careless. However, don't take him at face value. He is the enemy; don't ever forget how crafty he is. You must be even craftier. Do not fall prey to him.

The box beneath the bundle contains slippers to protect your steps upon this impossible journey we've set for you. It also contains two vials…the lavender one is to be used to purify your body on the day of Samhain before you go to do battle with the creature. The green one contains a potion that you are to drink when you are on your way down to the creature's lair. Once you are with him, you must beguile him and procure from him a willing kiss. When he has tasted your lips he will be weakened, and you can make sure he doesn't go free. The incantation you use to bind him must be of your own choosing; if we were to supply it he would know.

We have faith in you, my dear descendant. All who came before

you stand with you now. Carry us in your heart. Never doubt yourself, for you are the Guardian of Misty Hollow.
    Lovingly, Harriet.

"I've got to get him to kiss me," she moaned. "Harry!" she protested. "Really?" The chandelier above tinkled merrily. Nora groaned. "This potion of yours had better work," she warned the spirits, "Because I am not strong enough to resist his...charm for very long." Having made the admission, she paused. "Charm...the locket," she murmured. "All the strength of the chain of Guardians is in the locket...." She looked at the cloak. "And stealthily I shall be covered, and demurely allow him to think he's won...." Again the crystals moved. "I see," she mewled. "Okay, Hail Caesar."

She rose from the floor and gathered her arsenal. Once she was back down in her bedroom, she placed the items in her bathroom, where prying eyes would not see and a nosy elf wouldn't dare go. But just in case, Nora placed her first wards to secure the room. Being a beginner, her spell was simple and direct. But by the will of the powers that be, it worked.

~*~

Samhain swept in, cold and gray and blustery. The old cottage creaked and groaned as the wind tore at every board and timber. The trees moaned as the wind crossed over and through the barren branches. Nora stayed secluded in her chamber, fasting and preparing mentally for what was about to happen. Liam had come to her door twice and asked if she needed anything. She had denied him access, and sent him away with a curt no, thank you. Robyn was moving about heavily down in the kitchen, having what she was sure was the elf's version of a tantrum. And somewhere deep under the house, Nora knew Byntwig had taken refuge. She suspected he too had a means of cloaking, and being closer to dirt made things easier for him. He would not give her away; he would make the wards hold. As long as he could give her just enough time.

She spent most of the day in bed, conserving her energy, protected from detection by the last waning surges of Winnie's bolstering of the original wards. For this plan to work, Nora knew that she had to let the shields drop dangerously low. When the shadows gathered in the late afternoon, she rose from the bed and moved to the bath to use the first vial and purify her body. She half expected the ointment to stink, but was pleasantly surprised to find the fragrance appealing. She used it on skin and hair alike, wanting the full effect, and found that it left her feeling tingly and fresh. She dried herself and gazed into the reflection of the steamy bathroom mirror.

With more care than she'd ever taken in preparing for even a date with Daniel, she began to prepare for her encounter with Garnel. He would be expecting a mouse, and she didn't wish to disappoint him. Never having used many cosmetics, she found that not having to rely on them now was a good thing. The dark circles that she'd allowed to form under her eyes were still visible, if not as pronounced. Her hair, once dried, lay rather softly, but didn't look like the fancy cut that Connie was known to wear. She looked at her face, plain and unadorned, but soft and innocent. The perfect sacrificial lamb, she mused. She hoped it would be enough to entice the Garnel into a false sense of victory.

The mauve gown felt like butterfly wings over her skin,

and she resisted the urge to put on modest undergarments. This was no time for modesty, and the Garnel would be expecting her to either try to battle him or to surrender to her darkest, most secret desires of the flesh. She cinched up the gown and studied her own reflection. In spite of the fact that she had no makeup on, or perhaps because of it, she looked like a stereotypical tempting virginal sacrifice. She added the locket just before she wrapped herself in the cloak, and pulled up the hood to cover her head.

    Silently she opened the door, taking care not to let the hinges creak. Listening, she waited until she was certain that both Liam and Robyn were where they would not hear or see her. On softest steps she crept down the stairs, holding the cloak tightly about her, one step at a time until she reached the foyer. The cloak was keeping her stealthily hidden from her so called protectors, just as she had known it would. She heard Liam and the elf in the kitchen, talking about the impending battle and making plans for how to save the world if Nora failed. Part of her wished she could tell them not to worry, but she knew it was best to let them fret, as Garnel was feeding off their fears.

    She was just a few short steps from the front door. The moments stretched like hours as she inched her way across the hardwood floor with catlike footsteps. Slowly she opened the door, praying the old hinges wouldn't give her away, and stepped across the threshold. Without second thoughts she moved down the steps of the front porch, slipping into the shadows of the gathering evening, the cloak covering her movements. There would be no trick or treaters here. There were no neighborhood children to fret about wandering in and upsetting the plan or being put in danger. Liam and Robyn wouldn't know she was missing until it was over, one way or the other. She could feel that the old troll was aware of her, and using his own magic to help her plan along.

Feeling extraordinarily sure for the first time in her life, Nora headed down the path that would take her to the shortcut to the swamp. She didn't go down the hillside through her own garden, where the men in the kitchen might see her. Something told her that Garnel would be waiting, expecting her. She was aware he would know she was coming, and that she was alone. Keeping humble, she made sure her head was bowed in a sign of submission. *Don't get cocky*, she warned herself once more. *The fate of the world is in your hands, Nora Belfry.*

The shadows deepened as dusk fell upon and covered the meadow and the swamp in its darkening blanket. She didn't think about the hillside cottage. Her mind was on what she was about to say to the creature awaiting her. *Let me be convincing*, she prayed silently as she raised the vial to her lips and drank its contents. *Hail Caesar*, she sighed inwardly. She placed the vial in the crotch of a tree she passed on her way. She could smell the dank odor of musty waters and rotting vegetations. Taking one more deep breath, she committed herself to the execution of the dire strategy.

"Garnel," she called softly.

"I'm here." His voice sounded like it was coming from everywhere. Nora wasn't certain if it were his doing or the potion.

"I've come," she said, submissively. "You win." She found it easy enough to feel dejected and broken. They were feelings she was used to, feelings she could wrap herself in and not give herself away. Feelings that would be the undoing of the creature she was about to do battle with.

He moved closer, out of hiding and into the open. "And you are in agreement with my offer?"

"What choice do I have?" she said in a pitiful tone. "I don't want to die." That was easy to say; it was truthful. "Take me."

"A wise choice," he praised, coming even closer.

She pulled back her hood from her face, and looked up at him with as much sadness as she could pull forth. "I beg of you one thing...."

"And that is?"

"Allow me to see you only in this form...," she whispered. "I don't think I could willingly kiss and be taken by...." She shuddered.

Moved by her honest admission of fear, Garnel took her face in his hands and tipped her chin upward. "Poor little creature," he murmured as he lowered his lips to hers.

Nora had dreaded this moment. Yet as it happened, she found that it wasn't nearly as unpleasant as she'd feared it might be. In fact, it was far more pleasant than the kisses of Daniel had ever been. Her lips parted and she freely allowed the Garnel to taste the sweetness she was allowing him to believe she was partaking in. Her hands moved as if they had an agenda of their own, snaking up the broad and firm back of the man-like creature. It was not her first kiss, but it was the one she'd most likely remember for the rest of her life. When it ended, she almost felt sorry for what was about to happen. She rested her head against his chest, a wave of dizziness enveloping her.

"I will not promise you forever," he told her softly. "It is not in my nature. However, I will pledge to you that you will not be disappointed, even if you have regrets."

She nodded.

"Let us stroll your garden," he suggested. "It's been far too long since I've been free."

Nora kept her face passive as she allowed him to lead her toward the wall and the lower gate and arbor arch. The dizziness was passing, and as she approached the wall, she felt a surge of power rush like fire in her veins. He released her from his embrace and said gently, "And now you must pass through the gate, and I will join you."

Her hand touched the wooden gate, swung it open, and without looking back, she said in a voice that was full of authority, "I don't think so." She let the gate fall into place. Turning, she placed her hands on her hips and said, "Time has come for you to return to your slumber."

The stone wall began to vibrate as the Garnel roared and moved to rush forward. It began to shine with a strange, unnatural light that came from its very depths. The Garnel cried out as the light and the energy of the wards returned to full strength and force. The entire moraine vibrated with the energy and power of the wards, and so did Nora.

"That's not possible," he roared. "You don't have the power or skill to restore the wards."

"Yeah, yeah," she mocked him. "So you and Robyn keep telling me. But guess what…you were both wrong."

Garnel suddenly became aware of an unpleasant taste within his mouth. "You tricked me!" he accused.

"Turnabout seems fair play to me." She crossed her arms.

"You tricked Winnie when she was feeling too cocky. I'm just returning the favor."

"How?"

"That's my secret," she preened. "Now, be a good little monster and return to your lair for another year's slumber. Oh, and by the way, don't expect me to be a pushover next year. You may have prevented me from being prepared for our initial tangle, but it'll never happen again. And in the future, you may address me as Guardian."

Garnel for a moment appeared to be conflicted; he wanted to roar, but another part of him urged him to laugh. That was the side that won, and he chuckled darkly. "I see," he mused. "Well, a fully-fledged Guardian is a much more interesting opponent than a weak little mouse could ever be." He bowed to her. "You've won this first battle, madam, but not without having lost some innocence." He looked at her with dark desires unmasked. "And you can't tell me you didn't want me."

"Wanting you and having you are two very different things," she advised. "I may be a virgin," she stated coldly, "but I'm not stupid."

"No, Nora Belfry, you are not stupid," he agreed. "But you did want me," he taunted. "I've had a taste of you, and the taste of me will long linger in your memory." He looked up at the clearing sky and the stars that were now beginning to shine. "What a lovely evening we could have made of it." His eyes met hers. "You're going to regret not waiting until I'd—"

"Yeah, yeah, yada yada." She waved him off. "Go to your lair and have your sweet dreams of what might have been.

Go on, go."

"I'll have my dreams," he assured her. "And you'll have your nightmares."

"Sleep well, Garnel," she said sweetly.

"I'll be back, Nora," he said warningly. "And next time I won't be as…generous. There'll be no offer of pleasures untold."

"We'll see." She gave him a wan smile, he turned, and she watched as he began to make his way back to the swamp. He paused only once, looked over his shoulder, winked, then smiled at her. She knew he was back in the swamp, back in his lair, when she heard his howl. "Sweet dreams, Garnel," she said before she turned to look at the cottage up the hillside.

Two figures were coming down, and she prepared to give them the news. There was a new Guardian in town. Reaching out her hand, she fired up the wards in the wall to their full extent, as well as the wards that protected the entire property and kept the Garnel prisoner of the Misty Hollow. The entire reach of the moraine shot up in part of the ongoing wards of protection that kept the portal that the Garnel had used to enter the world of man dormant.

Robyn came forward and gasped, "You can't…."

Nora smiled. "Wanna bet?"

Liam heard the howl in the distance and demanded, "What did you do?"

Robyn shook his head in disbelief. "But you can't!"

"My job," she said to Liam, before she addressed the elf. "Oh, but I can and I did, and I will continue to do what the Guardian of the Misty Hollow is expected to do."

"But you don't know how," the elf insisted, stomping a

foot.

Liam seemed to be the one who realized she wasn't dressed in her regular attire. "Where did you get these garments?"

"From Aunt Harriet," she said without reservation. "While Garnel may have tied Winnie's hands, he forgot that the Guardians have a long, well forged chain that goes very far back and is ongoing. *The Belfry witches have their way*; isn't that what you told me, Liam?"

"You shouldn't have faced it alone," Liam said, relieved that she was none the worse for her experience. He moved toward her, thinking to embrace her.

Nora held up a hand, preventing him from coming closer. She could still taste the Garnel, and didn't wish to share that with Liam. "What would you have done, had I shared my plan with you?"

"I'd have stopped you," he admitted. "It was foolish for you to risk this alone."

"Liam." Her voice softened and saddened. "You don't have the right to tell me what to do." She watched as his eyes filled with guilt. "I know you care about me, and I am grateful for that. Nevertheless, you don't have the right to make it more than what it is. I am now, and will always be, your friend and loving cousin." She clasped her hands before her. "But that is all we shall ever be." She stood closer to the wall and the flow of its ongoing energy, taking strength from it to say what she needed to…to free him and send him on his way. "I am thankful for your faith in me and for what you tried to teach me. But it's time that you return to your people. You have your life, and I have mine."

"Such wisdom," the dark Celt sighed. "It is true; I have

my own people, my own life waiting for me. But I would have gladly spent the last moments of reality with you." He bowed to her. "Blessed be, Guardian of the Misty Hollow. Long life and peace be yours."

Without another word he turned and headed to the path that would lead out of the Hollow. Nora had never asked how he had arrived, and she didn't think asking how he was going to return to Scotland was suitable. All she could do was watch him walk out of her life, and not beg him to stay.

She looked at Robyn when Liam was gone from sight. "Time for you to go too, Elf-boy."

"No pretty speeches between us," he said a bit frostily. "That is as it should be, I suppose."

"I won't forget you tried to help," she stated. "The peace that is between our people reminds intact."

"There's no love lost betwixt and between us, Guardian. In another hundred years...I may mellow," he suggested.

"Doubtful," she teased.

A moment later the surly elf was gone, and only Byntwig was left to bid her farewell. Taking a seat on the wall, Nora awaited the approach of the old troll mage. His departure was the one she wished she could delay. There was so much the old troll could teach her. He was smiling, and looking rather like a cat that'd eaten a cage of canaries. Leisurely he strolled until he reached the wall and he too took a seat.

"Lovely evening, isn't it, Guardian?"

"Yes," she agreed, looking up at the stars. "Lovely indeed, old mage."

For a few moments the two mages shared peace, then the troll glanced at her. "Was it terrible?"

"No," she said with a blush. "Not terrible." She began to giggle like a schoolgirl. "Not terrible at all."

"Interesting," he teased.

"Very," she quipped back with rosy cheeks.

Byntwig snorted. "It's been a pleasure working with you, Guardian." He hopped down from the wall. "A very great pleasure." He looked at her with the same expression Winnie used to. "I'm very fond of you."

"Nice working with you, Troll Master, and I am fond of you," she said formally. "You, sir, are welcome in the Hollow anytime you're passing through."

"Of course I am," he said proudly as he sauntered away. "I'm Byntwig, Master Mage of the Troll Kingdom."

They were all gone; the elf, the Celtic shaman, and the troll. The Garnel was back in its lair, and the world was safe for at least one more year. She had done it; she had saved the world. The girl who had been kept from knowing and learning the true nature of her being had conquered her fears and saved the world. And she'd done it her way.

Quietly she moved up the hillside and looked at the design of tiles and stones that made up the patio. She remembered the words that the elf and gypsy had her recite. With a wistful smile she uttered them once again. This time she clasped the locket as she did. "*Ddraig o fywyd; Gwrando fy ple; Gadewch i fy anwylyd siarad â fi.*"

A shimmering light filled the patio, and the images of Winnie, Harriet, Anna, and Agatha all appeared. Each of them seemed to be pleased, each for her own reasons. All four Belfry Guardians were in gowns much like her own. Nora smiled back. "I wanted to thank all four of you for showing me the way."

"I knew the power was always in you," Winnie insisted, looking embarrassed but proud. "I'm only sorry that I made this harder for you."

Harriet nodded. "You had only to trust in yourself."

"The Belfry line goes on," Anna agreed.

Agatha was not about to begin fawning over the girl. "Yes, yes, good work…but now the real undertaking begins. You must make up for lost time." She moved to a place in the circle of stones. "I had an Indian shaman to show me the way, and I passed my knowledge on to Anna, and she to Harriet." As she spoke the others joined her in standing in the stone circle. "The knowledge of the Guardians is now yours to own. You've won the right to be the keeper."

Eagerly the girl nodded. "I've a lot to learn, ladies…so let us get started." She moved to take her place in the circle of stones that formed the pattern on the ground. "Tis the night of the marriage of Day and Night, and your student is ready to learn."

"Blessed be," Agatha said, and the phrase was repeated by the rest of the Guardians.

Chapter 19

Weeks later the first snow lay on the ground. Nora was dressed in one of her beautiful vintage outfits that had been stored in the trunks belonging to other Belfry Guardians, prepared to join the family for Thanksgiving dinner at the home of her uncle John. It was the first time in a very long time that she'd even received an invite. When her parents had moved out of state, contact with the head of the family had seemed to be severed. Nora wondered if that was Uncle John's doing alone, or the influence of the Garnel.

Her little VW was still in the shop, and there seemed no way of knowing just when it would be done. Jake had more difficulty fixing the little car than anticipated. From parts being unavailable to more extensive damages than he'd foreseen, the little car was taking much longer than he'd promised. That, she was sure, was Garnel getting his last licks in.

With the VW out of commission, Nora had begun to depend on the vintage Model T in the garage. Pulling on a long, heavy canvas duster, Nora tied on a wide brimmed driving bonnet she'd found up in a hat box in the storage part of the attic. She carried a car blanket draped over one arm, having placed the packages she was bringing along in the car already. Nora locked up the house and proceeded to the garage where Tin Lizzy was warming up, but not without having turned to gaze at the house. "Creatures that human eyes don't see, keep my house and home safe for me." Knowing her wards were effective, she moved swiftly to the carriage house.

She pulled Tin Lizzy out of the garage, got out, and carefully locked the latch. She looked up at the falcon that watched her with steady eyes. "Keep a sharp eye on things, Rex, I leave everything here for you to keep safe," she told the bird. "I'll be back late." She settled herself in the driver's seat, placed the blanket over her lap, and adjusted the seat position. She was glad that Aunt Winnie had also been a woman of short stature, and that her specially designed leather seat-booster worked for Nora as well.

The roads had been cleared of snow at dawn, and now were easily traveled. The long winding drive had been cleared by the firm that Winnie insisted was the best she'd ever used. Nora pulled Tin Lizzy down the drive and out onto the main street at the end of her property. Nora was getting use to the honks and waves from other drivers whenever they saw the shiny red Model T, with the vanity plates reading Miss Lizzy. This morning, dressed in period garments, she was drawing even more attention. She settled back and decided to enjoy the drive into the city. It would take an hour or better to arrive at the mansion that was the homestead of the Belfry family.

~*~

The Belfry family home was one of the older, statelier homes in the old Kenilworth area. The family had resided at this address for well over one hundred and fifty years. Like many old moneyed families, the estate passed from father to the firstborn son. Yet, all the Belfry's connected to the estate considered it *home*. It was here that the extended family would gather for holiday events such as Thanksgiving, Christmas, and Easter…even for family weddings. Connie's wedding had been celebrated there, in a very grand style, just as her mother's had.

Connie had arrived with Daniel McGowan on her arm as her guest. It had caused a few brows to rise, but nothing was said. David had arrived solo right behind her, as if he'd timed his arrival with hers. The house was full of excitement, as there was a guest from the Scottish branch of the family arriving to spend the holidays. John the third, his wife, and children were there, as was Connie and David's mother Mary Kate. Connie was a bit upset that the visiting Scot was stealing a bit of her thunder of her promotion, but quickly covered her disappointment. Nothing was going to crack her carefully placed veneer in front of Uncle John if she could help it. She painted on a simpering smile and behaved like a proper lady. David Logan followed his sister's lead.

Connie grew bored and was watching the clock. It was nearly time for dinner to be served, and Nora had neither shown up nor called. Indignantly she marched over to John Belfry the second to complain. "I don't know how you can stand for this, Uncle John."

"Stand for what?" he asked, a bit distracted by bouncing a grandchild on his knee.

"Nora's rudeness," she stated in a voice loud enough for anyone who wished to overhear. "She hasn't bothered to call to say she's not coming." She pointed to the clock. "It's nearly time for dinner to be served, and she's not here."

John gave his niece a troubled glance. "I'm sure she'll be here," he said calmly, not wishing to upset his grandchild. "No need to fret."

"You're not going to hold dinner for *her*, I hope," Connie interjected hotly. "Some of us have schedules to keep."

John the third frowned at his cousin. "Then by all means, feel free to keep to them."

David put a hand to Connie's sleeve, as if warning her not to go too far.

A moment later the butler answered the door and greeted Nora warmly. "Happy Thanksgiving, Miss Nora."

~*~

"Happy Thanksgiving to you, Jules." She stepped in and handed off the large basket carrying the gifts to the man. "A bit nippy out there, isn't it?" she added with a smile. Removing the bonnet, she unfastened the duster and handed the outside garments to a maid, who was waiting for them. Smoothing her dress and placing a hand to her hair, she made sure her appearance was presentable. The butler returned her basket to her, and told her to go into the parlor where the family was gathered.

"I do hope you'll all forgive my tardiness," she said pleasantly as she entered the room. "Happy Thanksgiving, Uncle John, Aunt Martha, Aunt Mary Kate." She greeted the elders of the family first with poise and confidence. "Mother and Father send their holiday greetings."

John the third whistled low as he turned to glance at his cousin. "Well, look at you," he exclaimed. "You look wonderful, Nora."

Nora flashed a pleasant smile. "Why thank you, John." She continued into the room.

"You're late," Connie said, ignoring Nora's new found poise and elegant attire.

"Well, it couldn't be helped...car trouble," Nora said softly.

"If you got rid of that rattle trap VW—," Connie began, with David nodding in agreement.

"Oh, I didn't drive the VW," Nora interrupted her. "The bug is in the shop."

"In the shop," John the third questioned. "I was under the impression that you kept it in tip top shape."

"A case of vandalism; someone broke in and poured pepper into my gas tank," Nora shrugged, "Happened right after I moved into the cottage, and the mechanic is having a devil of a time undoing the damages." She was handing little boxes out to people as she spoke. "So, since I'm without my usual mode of transport these days, I've learned to depend on old Tin Lizzy." She placed the empty basket on the floor. "She's a joy to drive!"

"You drove that rust bucket here?" Connie glared at her. "To Kenilworth?"

"Lizzy may be vintage, but she's not a rust bucket. I'd challenge anyone to find one speck of rust on her," Nora stated firmly, not giving an inch, "And yes, I drove her here." The bell rang and the butler moved to answer it, "I'm not the last to arrive?" Nora inquired.

Uncle John slid his grandchild off his knee. "We've a guest arriving from our Scottish branch. Do try to be nice to him." He shot a glance of warning at Connie. "All of you." John moved toward the foyer. "Welcome," he said to someone coming toward him. "I'm your cousin, John."

"Liam Belfry." The man offered his hand in greeting to his distant cousin.

"Welcome Stateside," John greeted him in return. "Come in and meet some of the rest of your family."

"The Euro trash?" Connie gasped.

Liam was commenting, "I saw this amazing car parked in the drive, and had to stop to admire it. I've only seen one other like it. Who does it belong to?"

Nora looked at the man standing in the archway, and her heart skipped a beat. Dressed in the most fashionable and expensive suit stood Liam, looking like a British jet setter. "Liam?" she whispered. She was aware of Connie's glare directed her way.

"My brother Edward's only child," John said softly. "A nice, quiet girl," he added, giving Connie a warning glance. Uncle John turned to his guest. "My father's sister left her estate to our niece here, and part of the estate is a wonderful mint Model T that she named Tin Lizzy. Hence her old fashioned outfit." He motioned Nora to come closer. "Nora, this is our guest from Scotland, and the forges there. Liam Belfry."

"They know each other," Connie protested loudly. "I saw him out at the Hollows when I went there to...visit."

Nora blushed and turned to her uncle. "Liam and I are acquainted," she agreed. "It's lovely to see you again, cousin."

"And you. I should have known it was Tin Lizzy." The Scot bent toward her and kissed her cheek gently. "Thank you so much for your hospitality during my brief stay earlier this year." He turned to Uncle John. "I was here on business. Nora allowed my companion and I the hospitality that Winnie had offered when I was corresponding with her, shortly before her passing. Winnie and my grandmother were very close, you know."

John gazed at his niece. "Did she? Well done." He escorted the visitor to meet others.

~*~

Daniel stood beside Connie, staring at Nora's attire, her new hairdo, and her unusual poise. "What happened to her?" he asked quietly. "I've never seen her so...animated."

"She's gone around the bend, if you ask me," Connie glowered, and moved closer to her younger cousin. "What kind of get up are you wearing?" Connie snarled at Nora.

~*~

Coolly the younger woman turned and gave her cousin a raised brow. "You don't like my outfit?"

"It looks like a cheap costume," Connie said a bit louder, expecting backup from other family members. "But then you never did understand quality."

Nora saw disappointment in Connie's eyes when David didn't join in the taunt immediately.

Liam had returned to be closer to where Nora stood. "I think it's charming," Liam offered. "Why, it's the height of fashion right now, with the Victorian craze in London and Paris." His words upset Connie more than Nora's poise. "Very chic."

"Old clothes from an attic are not…," Connie argued, "acceptable attire for a formal Belfry family dinner. I would think someone from the Continent would know that." Nora could see that Connie still didn't like Liam, and she was unexpectedly glad.

"Are you the fashion police in my home now?" Uncle John asked, handing off his grandson once more to his daughter-in-law. Connie turned to stare at him, her mouth agape. Nora had never heard him address Connie with such tenseness in his tone.

"I think you look charming," Aunt Martha gave her opinion.

Connie's mother nodded in agreement. "That dress suits you," she complimented. "I always said you reminded me of Aunt Winnie…."

"Living out in that hovel has addled your brains," Connie snapped. "Old second hand clothes from an attic; you look like a joke."

"Vintage garments," Nora corrected gently. "And couture at that. Care to read the label, dear?" She saw Connie taken aback by her newfound self-assurance.

Uncle John gave both his nieces an odd gaze; Nora could see him wondering if he'd missed something all these years. Had Connie always spoken so callously to Nora? Had he overlooked Nora's quiet nature and mistaken her for being insignificant or inconsequential? His thoughts troubled him. "Constance," he addressed her stridently. "Apologize to your cousin Nora at once."

Connie's face blanched, but her eyes went darker. "I'm sorry," she said, without the apology reaching her eyes.

Uncle John shook his head, looking angrily at the one who up until now had been his favorite niece. "What is the matter with you?" he demanded. "Why are you going out of your way to be so rude to Nora?"

"She's upset with me because I won't sell the Hollow," Nora said firmly and honestly. "She thinks that it's unfair that I inherited the estate, and believes that the entire thing should be sold and the proceeds distributed among the heirs, and that she should also make a nice big fat commission on the sale of the property."

Connie glared at Nora, unable to speak for a moment. "That land could be put to better use," she argued.

"That's family land, Constance!" Uncle John struggled for breath. "We don't sell family land."

Connie rolled her eyes. "Family land? It's only Aunt Winnie's shack in the woods. It's little better than a hovel, and should be condemned."

Daniel wisely stepped back, not wishing to be a part of an argument he could see Connie wouldn't win. Nora wondered if there was something more about the property that he was aware of that he'd not shared with Connie. His actions made her suspicious. *Once a snake, always a snake*, she reminded herself. *And they deserve each other.*

John blinked. "Who are you?" he asked in disbelief. "That house was and is a landmark, I'll have you know." He shook his head from side to side, trying to understand her anger and spitefulness. "It's on the National Historical Homes register. And it's been in the family since it was built, Constance. It's an Illinois architectural gem! It was designed by Frank Lloyd Wright just prior to his move into the Prairie School style.

Shack, indeed. And that land has been in the family since just after the Civil War!"

Seething, the dark haired girl in the red power suit took a new path of attack. "Then it should belong to *you*...you're the head of the family, not *Nora*." Thinking she'd found a way to wound Nora, she smiled. "Kick her out."

Nora stood impassively, waiting to see what Uncle John would say. He stared. "I'll do no such thing," he said at last. "And you'll never make such a suggestion again."

"She doesn't deserve it," Connie blurted out. "She's nothing, a little nobody! No one in the family likes her! She's a little better than a charity case." Her eyes turned on Nora, and the quiet Guardian sensed the influence of the lightly slumbering Garnel, something she intended to bring to an end...but not here, not now. "Why should she have it? Why should she have anything? She's not one of *us*!"

The room had gone rather silent. Nora could see that Uncle John and Aunt Martha were stunned by Connie's uncontrolled outburst. Aunt Mary Kate looked like she wanted to crawl under a rock, and even David had the good sense to appear taken aback. Liam moved closer, letting her know that he'd support whatever tact she took. At the moment Nora was more concerned about Uncle John than herself, as he had gone red-faced with anger.

John the third answered for his struggling father. "Because it was Aunt Winnie's wish that Nora have it. Father, are you all right?" He was concerned how this was affecting his father's health. Nora suspected that Uncle John was not as well as he wanted everyone to think he was.

"Connie, you're going too far," John the third warned.

"It's no skin off your nose that Winnie did a kindness to Nora. Nora, after all, has been always there for Aunt Winnie. I know for a fact that neither you, David, nor I were." He tried to sound reasonable. "You and David and I were raised in the laps of luxury. Would you deny some of that to Nora?"

"Yes, I would," Connie answered. "Why shouldn't I? Why should she rate anything more than a passing, pitiful thought? Her parents are little better than paupers."

"Because she's a *Belfry*," Uncle John answered. "And for your information, young woman, her father is my brother! He is not a pauper." Nora feared this was too much for her uncle, who was obviously not in the best of health. She'd seen symptoms like this before, in her father.

Nora had remained silent, but now spoke up. "Connie, you never liked going out to the Hollow, and I know I'm not your favorite person in the world, but there are things in this life that are not under your influence or your control. The Hollows is one of them." Her tone was calm and logical, trying to defuse the situation. The last thing she wished for was Uncle John being made ill. "Aunt Winnie was very generous in all her bequests." She didn't cower, but held her ground. "As was Grandfather. No one protested when he left you the ski cabin up in Iron Mountain." She reminded her cousin of the one-time family cabin that was now off limits to anyone but Connie.

"Perhaps I should have," Uncle John seethed.

Connie's eyes opened wide at the suggestion. "But, you *like* me," she objected. "You've never liked Nora...."

The words were meant to wound, but they hit the wrong target. Nora lowered her lashes and kept silent; Liam's hand went to her elbow, giving silent support. Uncle John swallowed hard. "Did I honestly give you all that impression?" He looked to his wife. "Did I?"

Aunt Martha went very still. "John...." She hesitated to answer.

~*~

John the third answered for his mother. "I'm afraid we both have." He glanced at the lovely, poised, and tranquil young woman most members of the family had ignored standing with the member of the family from across the pond. "We all sort of took dear little Nora for granted. She never made a fuss, or demanded attention, and we just ignored her. I'm so sorry, cousin."

~*~

Daniel appeared more and more uncomfortable. "I think perhaps I should go," he suggested. "This seems a family matter; David, would you see your sister home?"

Connie latched onto his arm. "Don't go." It was not a request, it was a demand. "I need you here."

Uncle John looked stunned. "How long have you two been carrying on?"

The hand on Daniel's sleeve slid off and dropped to Connie's side. "It's not what you think," she said. Nora could see her cousin trying to figure a way out of what was about to become a large mess.

Looking past her to Nora, Uncle John asked, "Am I mistaken?"

"No," Nora sighed, no longer protecting what she thought was her pride. "Connie and Daniel have been interested in each other since before he and I were together." Connie gave

Nora a murderous glare, but Nora didn't buckle. "I have no reason to protect your secrets anymore."

David moved to his mother's side, fearful of the noose tightening on him next.

"You were married," Uncle John accused.

Uncle John's disappointment in Connie was crushing to him. Nora placed a hand on his arm. "Uncle John, that's all water under the bridge," she soothed. "I bear neither of them any ill will. I am long over any hurt they caused me."

John whispered to her, "I blamed you...."

"I know," she said gently. "But you didn't have all the facts. And I couldn't give them to you, not then and not now."

"You should have told me," he protested. "I'm your uncle...."

"Why?" she asked with a sad smile. "Would it have done any good?"

John Belfry the second nodded, "Indeed."

Aunt Martha murmured, "When Edward left and asked you to look after Nora...." Her tone was bitter. "You told him that she was more than capable of looking after herself. Why would she have come to you?"

Nora patted her uncle's arm. "I'm not your daughter," she reminded him. "I'm only a niece, just like Connie."

John the third shook his head. "You're nothing like Connie; you never were. I see that, now."

"It doesn't matter," Nora insisted. "I'm happy with who I am." She looked over at Connie, who was standing beside Daniel. "I just wish you were happy with who I am as well."

Mary Kate Logan, having listened, spoke up at last. "Edward chose to live his life without all the trappings that *we* think of as being normal...things we have taken for granted. He raised Nora without the luxuries that our children became accustomed to," she admonished her children. "And for which they have never been grateful. I am ashamed of you both."

Uncle John sighed and put one arm about Nora. "I owe you an apology," he said grimly. "I never meant to treat you differently, and I'm sorry I took your good nature for granted."

Nora glanced about the room. "Look at us," she admonished lightly. "We're getting downright maudlin, and our visitor here is going to think we're a very black spot on the family name," she teased.

Liam, who most of the others in the room had forgotten was there, gave her a smile. "Oh, this is nothing compared to some of the antics back home." His face was passive. "Makes me homesick for one of my father's and his sister's donnybrooks."

Nora patted her uncle's back. "Let's get back to having a pleasant Thanksgiving."

"Dinner is served," Jules announced.

"Thank God," Aunt Martha muttered, a mutter echoed by Aunt Mary Kate.

Liam sauntered over to Nora, extended his arm, and waited for her to decide. Lightly she placed her hand to his sleeve. He patted her fingers lightly, giving her an understanding gaze before leading her into the dining room.

Once seated, Aunt Mary Kate commented, "Nora, that's a lovely locket. Where did it come from?"

"Aunt Agatha," Nora said.

"More hand me downs?" Connie asked coldly.

"In a way," Nora said, too cheerfully for Connie. "It was Agatha's first. She wore it in the family portrait that Brady did. She gifted it to Anna, who then handed it down to Harriet, who then in turn passed it on to Winnie, who left it to me."

"It's a lovely tradition," Aunt Mary Kate said. "A Belfry woman's tradition."

"A spinster's tradition," Connie whispered. "Thank God she didn't give that cursed trinket to me."

~*~

After dinner, Uncle John asked Nora to join him in his study while the other ladies went to the music room. When she entered, he asked her to shut the door and take a seat.

"I've talked to your father," Uncle John started the conversation.

Nora nodded. "Daddy said you called, a few weeks ago." She settled into one of the chairs. "But he didn't say what you two talked about. I assumed it was between you, and that's where I left it."

John leaned back in his chair. Nora wondered why he'd given up a chance for one of the cigars he was so proud of, and port wine with the other men. "I haven't been well," he said quietly. "My doctor informs me that a lifetime of abusing my body has caught up to me. And that faults that are inherited have decided to rear their ugly heads."

"Uncle John...." Nora leaned forward. "Is there anything I can do?"

John studied her for a moment. She wasn't sure what was racing in his mind. "Thank you," he answered. "That you would even extend such an offer after the way I treated you, and your parents...." He shook his head. "Did you know your father didn't wish to work in the family business?" He waited, and Nora wondered how to answer. "He didn't," her uncle continued, not waiting, and letting her off the hook as it were. "Your father had a great deal of talent as an artist, and as an architect, but my father insisted that he had to work for the company. And then he didn't even allow Edward to work in the design department, he forced him to work in accounting." Nora was aware, but she'd never heard her uncle say a single word about it before. "And I backed the old man, all the way." He frowned. "I always backed the old man. I never gave a thought to how it affected my poor brother." His face was a mask of shame. "I even had the gall to think he was faking it when he first got ill. You were a child, and I doubt you recall the terrible bout of scarlet fever.... You were sent to spend time with Winnie…your parents didn't want you to be exposed to the illness. It weakened your father's heart."

"They explained it to me when I got older," Nora said. "Then Daddy needed an operation when I was twelve, and the insurance wouldn't pay for it…and he refused to ask you or Granddad. He sold some of his bonds, and part of the ones meant to cover my college tuition, to pay the cost."

"Had we known…." John's voice caught in his throat as tears welled in his eyes. "Had we realized."

"Water under the bridge," Nora said softly.

"I had no idea he'd used so much of his own money, or his stocks," John said. "I wasn't interested enough to find out. Like Connie, I was embarrassed by his choices…his house, his life…his wife."

"Uncle, don't."

"When our father died, I thought that his treatment of Edward was because he thought Edward was a slacker, and didn't hold up his end of working for the family." Her uncle continued. "It never occurred to me that he hadn't been fair to Edward, or to you. I never gave thought to how he had made his bequests. How he had shown favoritism to Johnny, to Connie and David, and had barely given a single thought to you." He shrugged. "When Winnie left the Hollows to you, I thought, fine, I don't have to deal with it. I mean, it's out there in the middle of nowhere! With you owning it, it was still in the family." He sighed. "Then I went to the doctor, and discovered that there's a history of heart trouble in the family." He patted his chest. "My old ticker is working against me. I called your father, and we cleared the air between us."

"I'm glad to hear it," Nora said. "It always troubled Daddy that you and he were at odds."

"I'm going to make sure that he and your mother are taken care of," John promised. "I know it's late in the game, but I want to try and make up for some of the bad blood. I told my broker to buy back your father's stocks and send them to him." He shook his head. "Connie's remark about your parents being little better than paupers...."

"I'm sure that your outreach will make Daddy very happy. He always admired you."

"Did he?" John shook his head. "I wonder why...I never gave him reason to. I wasn't a very good brother. I never supported him; he'd have been better off with a different brother."

"That's not what Daddy says," she told him. "Daddy says that if it weren't for you, Belfry Industries wouldn't have come as far as it has. That you saved the company for future generations. We are still a name to be trusted, and the business is still here, and that's thanks to you."

John looked relieved. "That's good to hear." He smiled. "Johnny is taking over most of the day to day stuff," he explained. "And I'm going to be taking it a bit easier."

"You and Aunt Martha should take a trip west and visit Mom and Daddy," she suggested.

"It's in the planning stage." He held out his hand to her. "If you ever need anything, Nora...."

"Oh, I'm more than well taken care of," she assured him. "The Belfry women are very good at investing, and I love living at the Hollows."

"Still, if you ever have need...."

She squeezed the hand that had been extended. "I'll not be afraid to ask for help, should I ever have the need."

~*~

Hours later, Tin Lizzy was nestled back in the stall of the garage. Rex squawked in recognition when Nora locked up the garage. She looked up and praisingly said, "Good bird, pretty bird." Then, carrying her empty basket, she walked to the front door of the cottage. The woods were quiet, and the meadow and moraine were at peace. The wards held, and the moraine's energy fully energized the wall. Its energy signature could be seen by her.

Once inside she discarded her duster, bonnet, and basket. The lights, on timers, had come on, and the house was glowing warmly, welcoming her home. This was home, she reasoned, her home, just as it had been Winnie's, and Harriet's, and Anna's, and Agatha's. Just as it would be for future generations of Belfry Guardian, whoever that may be.

Pouring herself a sherry, she kicked off her shoes and moved to one of the big chairs that graced the room. Curling up just as she had when she was a little girl, Nora pondered the events of the day. She contemplated how much a part the Garnel's influence of Connie had played in the spectacle they'd made of themselves. She also wondered if a forthcoming engagement between Connie and Daniel might be on the horizon.

It amazed her that she hoped so; after all, they were so well suited to one another. She hadn't lied when she told her uncle she held no grudge. If they made each other happy, and stayed out of her life, she could be very supportive. There was no doubt it wouldn't be a local affair. Connie and Daniel smacked of the "Destination Wedding" types. Nora was sure she wouldn't be invited; as it was a second marriage for Connie, there wouldn't be the fanfare of a splashy white wedding in Belfry Mansion. Thank the Gods.

Nora sipped the smooth heady amber fluid in the fluted cordial glass. Its fire sped through her veins and gave gentle comfort. Nora knew, no matter what lay ahead, she could face it. The old influences that had shaped her life had given way to her new courage and outlook. The façade of the mouse was slipping quietly into the past, and she was emerging from her cocoon, a beautiful butterfly. It had taken twenty-eight years, but at long last she had bloomed. Part of her was glad it had taken this long, because the results were worth waiting for. Even all the old influences, and the obstacles of the past, had been worth it.

The few months she'd lived in the cottage had allowed

her to develop a sense of confidence, her own style, and settle into her own grace. While she didn't possess the panache and flair that were Connie's from the start, she did have her own brand of elegance and good taste. She wondered in the back of her mind what she'd have been like had she gone to a finishing school. In time, she had a feeling that the mouse would be forgotten, and the butterfly would be whom she was perceived as, and remembered for. It gave her peace to believe that. Nora also knew that her battles with the Garnel were not over; only this session was finished. While she couldn't let down her guard, she could relax, at least for tonight. Her world was at peace, and safe. Her father and her uncle were back on good terms, according to Uncle John, and he had even defended her. She knew that he and cousin John were on her side. Not even Connie's jealous tantrum could mar this day. She was finally feeling accepted as part of the family. She was confident, too, in the way her study of the family Guardians was coming along. Her own use of magic was improving.

The phone rang, and Nora answered, "Misty Hollow Cottage, Nora speaking."

"Liam here." The faint Scottish accent perked a bit. "I was wondering if you'd care to have dinner with me."

"I just did," she reminded him, the sherry making her feel a bit giddy. "Or had you forgotten?"

He chuckled gently. "I mean just you and me. Not the entire warring horde we are related to."

"It sounds very pleasant," she murmured as she sipped her sherry. "How about you come out to the Hollow and I fix you dinner?"

"You cook?" he asked, sounding mystified...she knew he was teasing. She'd cooked for him several times during his stay after she'd banned the elf from her kitchen.

"Very well," she said proudly. "If I do say so myself."

"How old fashioned of you," he teased. "When and what time?"

"When is best for your schedule?" she inquired. "I have no idea of how long a stay you're planning here in the States. I'm sure you're on a tight schedule."

"My time is my own now," he assured her. Nora found her heart racing; could that be possible? "How's tomorrow?"

"Tomorrow I'll be putting up holiday decorations. It's a family tradition," she said offhandedly.

"Need a helping hand?" His voice went husky. "I'm very good at holding ladders!"

"Help is always appreciated," Nora assured the man on the other end of the phone, fearful that she sounded much too excited, and didn't want to give the wrong impression.

"When will you be starting?" he asked gently.

"I'll be pulling the garland out of the attic storage at ten," she advised.

"Ten, it is. Until then...." He paused. "I'm looking forward to this, Nora."

"Me too," she said softly. "Good night, Liam." Hanging up, she heard a soft howl in the distance, and shivered. "Go to sleep, Garnel," she said softly before taking another sip of sherry. "I don't need or want your interference! You've caused me and mine enough trouble this day."

Chapter 20

Liam insisted on carrying the heaviest boxes down the stairs for her, and Nora allowed it without an argument. Her mother had told her never to argue with a man willing to do a chore. He had arrived at ten just as promised, and was dressed in casual attire, ready to work. They traded stories of family history while they worked, more pleasant stories than he'd heard the day before, touching on the traditions of the seasons. Liam took charge of the schlepping and heavy lifting, and Nora was beginning to enjoy his company. Neither brought up the first time they'd met and spent together prior to the defeat of the Garnel.

"I thought you handled that situation last night," he told her, "with a great deal of grace."

"Uncle John didn't need what Connie was trying to do. He's not well," Nora replied, still thinking about her cousin's jealous fit. "But I'm glad you were there, offering silent support."

"Always," he said with a smile. "Now, let's get to this!"

By three in the afternoon they were finished with the outside decorations and the inside trimmings. Even the artificial tree that Winnie had purchased so she didn't have to kill a living tree had been put up. Nora tapped the light switch and the old fashioned bulbs came alive with gentle laminations. Nora turned the dial on the dimmer for just the right touch of ambiance.

"It's beautiful," she said.

Liam placed an arm casually over her shoulder. "Indeed it is."

Leaning into him, she sighed. "Winnie loved the holiday season."

His arm constricted gently, pulling her closer till his chin rested on her head. "And you?"

"Oh, I love all holidays, but I think Christmas time was always my favorite," she admitted, not rushing to pull away.

"And what do you want for Christmas, darling Nora?" he whispered.

Shyly she gazed up, and for a moment she had no answer. "Happiness."

Rich chocolate eyes studied her. "Are you happy now?" His free hand came up under her chin.

"Yes," she nodded, keeping her gaze locked with his. "I'm happy that you're here."

Liam stroked her chin. "I'm glad," he admitted with mischief. "Because I intend to try to keep you happy, Nora Belfry."

"How can you?" she inquired softly. "You're still the Chovihano of the Fillip, the shaman of the People of the

Horse, aren't you? And your people are waiting for you.... And don't you have someone...special waiting?"

"I only have you," he promised as his lips moved to hers. "If you'll have me."

Nora didn't expect to feel the earth move beneath her; she didn't expect the wave of thrilling exhilarations that sped through her. She looked breathlessly at the man as the kiss ended. "That was nice," she whispered.

"That's just the beginning, Nora, my love," he promised. "I've waited a lifetime for just the right woman. Who knew she'd be a distant cousin?"

"Liam," she pulled back, suddenly remembering who and what she was. "I don't think—"

"Stop," he said gently. "I know every argument you're going to make against this."

"I don't think so," she told him with a sad laugh. "There's things about me," she warned. "Things you've no idea of."

He took her hand. "I knew from the moment I stepped into the parlor, dressed like a Celtic gypsy nightmare, challenging you to face me."

"Liam, don't," she pleaded.

"You don't believe in love at first sight?" he asked with a soft smile.

She looked deeply into the dark pools of brown; he wasn't playing a game, and she moaned softly. "It's not that." She turned away, trying to think of a way to explain why she couldn't commit to any relationship.

"Or is it you're worried that I'll run?"

The question struck her like a brick wall. She turned, wide eyed. "What did you say?" How was it he knew what she had been thinking?

He had taken a seat and was watching her. "We call it a touch o' the fae," he said, his accent thickening.

"What?"

"The gift," he continued. "We call it being fae, or being touched by the fae, on the other side o' the pond...or at least in our branch of the family."

"You too?" her voice was barely audible.

Giving her a wicked smile, he rested his elbow on the arm of the chair and his chin in his hand. "Aye," he nodded. "Not perhaps as powerful as the Belfry Guardian, but I have the gift." He smiled wickedly. "I told you there was a long heritage of witches and wizards in the family."

"Why didn't you tell me about you before?"

He winked. "Because I didn't believe I had a right, and we only had eight weeks in which to live. And I was under the impression that I was promised in marriage if the world didn't end."

She turned away, trying to clear her mind, finding that looking at her handsome relation set butterflies fluttering in her stomach. "This isn't happening," she said aloud.

Liam chuckled again. "That's what I was thinking yesterday."

Nora moved to the little table that held the sherry and poured one. She downed it quickly, and nearly choked on the liquor as it slid down her throat. Liam rushed to her side and poured her a glass of water from the decanter on the tray.

"Now, now," he advised. "No need to be drowning yourself in sherry," he teased gently. "Surely you're aware of the long heritage in the family."

"Only the lineage of the aunts," she sputtered. "I had no idea there were any male members of the family who have this."

"It doesn't happen often," he admitted. "Only once every few generations...and for a time we had to keep it very hush hush. Fear of witches, you know; well, actually, what the church did to those they claimed to be witches."

Calmer, and with the coughing spasm over, she looked at him. "Why are you telling me this now?"

"If I tell you, do you promise not to laugh?"

Nora frowned. "Do I look like I'm about to laugh?"

"No," he said curtly. "You look about ready to crack heads open."

Nora snorted. "Really?"

"Me mum told me...," he said quietly. "Oh, not about you by name, but she said I'd find my true love, a fae touched lass who would turn my world upside down and inside out." He captured her hands and held them close to his chest. "She said I'd see eyes the color of forest moss, and would fall into them, never to be free." He smiled. "She'll be very happy to hear how right she was. When I returned to the People of the Horse, I asked to be freed so I could return to you." He chuckled. "And it was a good thing Megan, the girl I was pledged to, did not want to marry me. She's in love with a farmer. We've both been released from the pledge. And a replacement shaman was chosen."

"We don't know each other," she protested. Motioning him to be seated, she poured out her tale of what had happened in his absence. She was standing directly in front of him as she finished. "And that's why, much as I love the idea of being with you, I can't. I have to put my duty as Guardian of Misty Hollow above everything." She looked at him with earnest eyes. "Do you understand?" He shook his head, and she moaned, "What part?"

"The part where you think a Guardian has to be celibate." Reaching out a hand, he pulled her to his lap. "Where did you get such a foolish idea, woman?"

Nora whispered, "All the Guardians here have been single ladies."

"Well, just because these four who came before you weren't married doesn't mean that others couldn't be," he argued. "Is it written in stone?"

Nora stared. "Not that I know of," she answered. "But I'm still learning."

"I know for a fact that Winnie wasn't celibate." Liam placed his arms about her. "Besides...." His eyes danced with merry mischief. "Just think of the fun of telling old Garnel that you've a sweetie! That the sweetie is me! It will drive the creature to distraction!"

Closing her eyes, Nora rested her head on his shoulder. "You're a sick, twisted man, Liam Belfry."

"I love you, too," he said quietly. "We'll have us a whirlwind and very public romance...and marry come the spring."

"Spring?"

"Aye," he said firmly. "I'm thinking May first."

"Beltane?"

He nodded. "Very Celtic, don't you agree?"

"You have this all planned out?" she asked, still resting against him. "Without even asking me what I thought?"

"Yes."

"Fine," she sighed. "But we have to live here."

"Agreed." He began to seek her lips.

~*~

The family heard the engagement announcement on Christmas day. On New Year's Eve the couple entertained for the first time. When spring came few could recall a time when Liam and Nora had not been a couple. Her parents and his flew in for the nuptials that took place in the garden of the cottage, with only family and close friends in attendance. After the guests had departed and the hired staff had cleared out, the bride and groom walked arm in arm down to the garden wall.

"Are you happy, me darlin'?" he asked as they strolled side by side.

"More than I ever believed was possible in this life," she said. "Are you?"

"Yes," he told her truthfully. He paused as they moved closer to the wall. "I can feel it," he told her. "That surge of energy."

"That's only part of what keeps the Garnel imprisoned," she stated.

He took a seat on the wall. "How deeply do you think he sleeps?"

"Not nearly as deeply as I would wish. I haven't learned how to put him into a deep sleep just yet, Aunt Harriet could make him sleep for years at a time." Her voice dropped low and dangerous. "And one should never underestimate him. Even in slumber he was able to affect Connie and David when we were kids, and into their adult lives. He influences them still, and from a distance."

"Can you feel him?"

She shook her head. "I never could."

Liam turned his gaze to the property beyond the wall. "At least he can't touch you, and ruin your happiness."

"Our happiness." She placed her arms around the shoulders of the man she'd married and murmured in his ear.

"Our happiness," he corrected as his hands reached out to her.

"All that I have I share with you," she whispered.

Liam nodded. "And all that I have is yours." Turning, he said, "I wish the other mentors could have been here."

She gave her new husband a wry smile. "Oh, I think they were." She pointed to shafts of light that seemed to dance in the meadow. "At least I hope so."

Liam chuckled softly. "Well then, Mrs. Belfry...." He stood up. "Are you ready to take the next step in what looks to be the adventure of a lifetime?"

"A lifetime of adventure," she mused. "Yes, Mr. Belfry, I'm ready."

Liam kissed her tenderly before he led her back to the little cottage that sat high on a moraine in the Misty Hollow. They both ignored the howl coming from the swamp.

The End

Author note; Thank you for having read this tale. Please remember to review on Goodreads.
Remember to look for my other titles as well.

Patricia M. Bryce is a short story author, novelist and cosplayer. She has appeared as Patricia M. Rose in the anthology, *Dreams of Steam: Gadgets*, edited by Kimberly Richardson and published by Dark Oak Press. Inspired and motivated by publication, she dusted off her fanfic and turned it into the original YA Fantasy series, Forged. When she's not busy writing, she's off being a 'playtron' (playing patron) up at Bristol Renaissance Faire during Faire Season. (That means she likes to play dress up still.)

Born in the City of Chicago, she hasn't strayed far from her roots. She is married, the mother of two grown children, and primary caregiver to her disabled husband.

In her own words; "Someone asked when I began to write. The simple answer is that I've written stories as long as I've known how to put two words together. From simple tales of our day, to the more fantastical tales of the Fae world, and even the world of young romance, and even the world of the paranormal."

You can learn more at https://www.facebook.com/PaisleyRose1

Or visit her site: http://patriciambryce.weebly.com/
My photo is by TGDavison Photography

CPSIA information can be obtained
at www.ICGtesting.com
Printed in the USA
FFOW04n1138220518
46817241-48980FF